GEMSTONE

A ZODIAC SHIFTERS PARANORMAL ROMANCE

ANN GIMPEL

Edited by

KATE RICHARDS

CONTENTS

GEMSTONE

A ZODIAC SHIFTER PARANORMAL
ROMANCE: GEMINI

Wylde Magick, Book One

By

Ann Gimpel

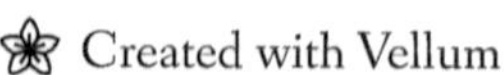 Created with Vellum

*N*iall's nothing if not charming with his Irish brogue and dashing good looks. Jaguar shifter and player to the core, he's a love 'em and leave 'em type. His job as a paramedic keeps him busy and offers under-the-table opportunities to splash a wee bit of magic around.

In a world where magic is all but invisible, Sarai and her family fly beneath the radar living on a small ranch outside Denver. She only takes her wolf form on the darkest nights when discovery is unlikely. Captured by a vampire consortium hellbent on world domination, she watches with horror as they siphon her power, diverting it to kill humans for sport.

An unnatural fog causes a ten-car pileup. Niall nearly chokes on the thick, malevolent power hanging around the accident site. Anger running just below boiling point, he takes his jaguar form and follows a scent track, making a discovery that changes everything. For once, he curses his curiosity and wishes he'd left well enough alone. Vampires are rising. Fueled by shifter magic, their evil threatens not just him but magic's very existence.

The constellation of Gemini depicts the twins, Castor and Polydeuces. Legendary dualistic zodiac sign, the discrepancy is actually between how the Gemini would like to be seen, and how he (or she) really is.

Curious, socially outgoing, and with a passion for novelty, Geminis are creative as all get out, but their follow-through sucks. The original commitment-phobes, Geminis have a tough time with romantic relationships because they're always on the prowl for a better offer.

Sirens blared, adding discordant notes to the squeal of spinning tires as the Medic One van careened around a corner. Adrenaline surged, and Niall MacLier pushed his right foot hard against the van's floor. He wasn't driving, but he wanted the ambulance to move faster. The radio sputtered, humming to life.

"Doc Hansen here. It looks bad. I'm ordering up another team."

Niall exchanged glances with Meredith West, the driver and a paramedic just like him. Her black hair fell in one long braid down her back, revealing the clean lines of her face and her deep-blue eyes. She had a hot little body, but she was also very married and had made it clear she wasn't interested in his cutesy suggestions they take a shag break in the back of the ambulance. She loved his Irish brogue, but that was where her fascination started—and stopped.

"What do you think?" he asked, without engaging the radio's push-to-talk switch.

She shrugged, and the van slewed around another corner, tires stuttering on rain-slick pavement. "About the other team?" At Niall's nod, she added, "Have the doc define bad."

Niall clicked the two-way. "How many injured?"

"Hard to say. The incident is still unfolding. At least six, though."

"Yeah." Meredith angled her head toward the mic. "By all means, send another team. We may be hot shit, but that's a lot for the two of us."

Niall dropped the radio back in its cradle. "How much longer till we get there?"

She tapped the navigation screen. "Maybe ten minutes. I swear, you're really dense when it comes to electronics."

Maybe because they didn't exist a few hundred years back.

He offered her a tight nod and undid his seatbelt so he could crawl into the back and get go-bags packed and ready. It removed the temptation to tell her what he really thought.

Or what he really was, which would be worse.

"Get back up here," Meredith shouted. "It's not safe."

"Sure and I'll be fine." He added a dollop of calming to his words. Last thing he needed was her giving him a hard time. Because her attention was glued to the road, he employed short jolts of magic to bring what he needed within easy reach.

Rain pounded on the van's roof. If the scene was as chaotic as he suspected it would be, he'd keep right on drawing power to save people. No one would notice the flickers of charged air, not in this downpour. And if they did, they'd chalk it up to a mini electrical storm.

As he stuffed supplies into duffel bags marked with a white cross and a caduceus, he wondered—again—if he'd done the right thing settling in Glenwood Springs, Colorado. It was the smallest place he'd ever lived, and people wanted to get up close and personal right away.

Except for Meredith.

He'd had a relatively simple time keeping to himself in New York and Los Angeles and Seattle and Denver, the four places he'd lived over the past couple hundred years since he crossed the Atlantic with a boatload of shifters just like himself.

They'd decided it was better if they spread out. America was a big place, and if they didn't settle on top of one another, perhaps they'd be able to conceal what they were. Magic had almost been their undoing in the

Old Country with the Church intent on shackling them to mute their ability. Burning or hanging followed on the heels of iron manacles.

He'd picked Glenwood Springs, a small community that butted up against extensive wilderness because he was sick of not being able to shift. If it was a mistake, it was one he'd jumped into with both eyes open.

Niall shivered. He made it a habit not to look back. Who the hell knew why sitting on the cold metal floor shook memories loose? The van lurched to a precipitous halt, accompanied by screeching brakes.

"Aye, and you'd drive better if you weren't sexually frustrated," he yelled in the general direction of the cab.

"Smarty pants," she retorted. "Look out a window. It's a fucking mess out there."

He latched the duffels around his shoulders, crawled to the back door, and opened it. Maybe it was opening the door that unlocked his senses, but screams and moans and the hot, coppery stench of blood blasted him. Along with it came foul magic. Lots of it, throbbing in primitive patterns that chilled him to his bones. He wanted to dig deeper, determine where it was coming from, but Meredith planted herself in front of him, arms extended. "Toss me one of those kits."

He jumped down and handed hers over. "Team or solo?"

She craned her neck. "Other van's not here yet. I say we split up." She keyed the mic to her communicator, and it chirped in his ear.

Resisting an impulse to rip the plastic earbud out, he said, "Fine by me, darling. I'm as close as your electronics," and took off at a run for the first overturned vehicle.

He waited for her to follow him, complaining about the endearment, but it didn't happen. He joined the group trying to free the driver from a smashed mini pickup. "One of you tell me what happened." He infused compulsion into the request, turning it into a demand.

"Not sure," a wraith-thin man with silver hair replied. "I mean, the weather was hideous, but all of a sudden this dense fog settled over us. I couldn't see two feet in front of me."

"Me, either," another man chimed in. This one was younger with reddish hair cut close to his head.

"I pulled over," the first man said. "Finding the side of the road was like reading braille. I overshot it. By the time I was parked, I heard cars smashing into one another."

"Pretty much the same for me," the younger man said. "I started to get out, but it sounded like bumper cars gone bad, so I stayed in my truck until I thought it might be safe."

While the men talked, Niall took advantage of their attention being elsewhere and bent back the metal holding the driver prisoner. If he was playing it by the book, he'd have retreated to the van for a backboard. Instead, he scanned the unconscious man with magic for spinal cord deformities. Once he was convinced he wouldn't cripple the man for life, he lifted him gently from the cab.

The lights of the second ambulance cut through fog and rain. Good, they could transport this guy to Valley View, Glenwood Springs' only hospital. By now, he was positive fell power was responsible for the wreckage spiraling around him, but he had lives to save.

"Could one of you flag that ambulance and tell them I've got one to go?" Niall asked.

Both men turned away, and Niall did more poking and prodding, encouraging the unconscious man to rejoin the land of the living. If he was awake and talking—and moving his extremities—no one would insist on a backboard and cervical collar.

"Arrgh, I feel like shit," the man moaned.

"'Twill be fine, mate. You banged your forehead on the windshield." Niall leaned close. "Your guilty no-seatbelt secret is safe with me."

The man's blue eyes widened. He probably wasn't much past eighteen, twenty at the outside. "Aw shit. Thanks. I was only going a couple blocks. Didn't think—"

Niall closed a hand over his shoulder. "'Tis all right. I skip mine when I shouldn't too."

"W-where you from?"

"Ireland."

The clomp of boots splashed over wet asphalt, and two men wearing paramedic uniforms rolled a gurney close, lowering it to ground level. Niall straightened. "He'll be fine. Nothing broken. Maybe a mild concussion. They can clear him in the ER."

"Want to help us load him?" The younger of the two paramedics asked.

"Sure, mate, but there's way more to do."

"He's right," the other paramedic said. "John and I have this. Get moving. We'll be back as quick as we can. Christ. What a mess. This is like a ten-car pileup."

"Yeah, and no one knows a thing, at least according to what the cops were saying over the radio," the other paramedic muttered. Turning to his coworker, he said, "You get his shoulders. I'll grab the legs."

Niall loped into the storm before they started to ask about his assessment and what he'd done or how he'd extricated the poor sod from his broken truck. He could lie, but it was easier not to have to answer at all.

It was hours past nightfall when he finally finished triaging the injured. Meredith slogged toward him, her wet jacket clinging to her like a second skin. Sodden bits of hair stuck to her wet face. "Ready to blow this popsicle stand?" She tried for jaunty, but she sounded trashed.

"Only if you let me drive." He held out his hand for the keys.

She fished them out of her slicker and tossed them his way. "No argument there, partner. I might fall asleep behind the wheel."

"Want me to drop you at home?" They reached the ambulance, and he pulled the passenger door open for her.

"It's against regulations, but yeah, that would be great. Hubby-boy can drive me back to the shop tomorrow to get my car."

He closed her door and walked around to his side, climbing into the cab. He'd fired the engine and headed for the west side of town where Meredith lived in one of the newer developments when she said, "I'm beat and not processing all that well, but did the whole mess we just left seem odd to you?"

Not odd at all. Just a few supernaturals throwing their weight around.

"Odd, how?" he probed, wondering what had tipped her off. Once humans found out about him and his ilk, it wouldn't be pretty. Last thing he wanted was a replay of his last years in County Donegal dodging clerics and the law.

Meredith dropped her face into her hands and dragged the heels of her palms down it. "I don't know. Odd. The weather was bad, but everyone relayed variations on the same theme. A mystery fogbank blew up out of nowhere and surrounded them." She shook her head. "It could be global warming, but I've lived here all my life and never heard of such a thing. Not that we don't get fog, but it thickens gradually, not all at once. And it never gets so dense you can't see anything, like this bunch claimed."

"Climate change is doing some unusual things," he murmured, intent on altering Meredith's version of reality. "Look at all the tornadoes and hurricanes and freak snowstorms."

She lowered her hands to her lap, staring at them. "Yeah. Maybe you're right."

"Only maybe?" he inquired.

"I guess you didn't feel it, huh?"

"Feel what? I was pretty busy. So were you."

"Something felt strange out there. Eerie. Like people were watching me, except I couldn't see them. Every time I looked, nothing was there." A nervous laugh rattled from her. "Don't listen to me. Not sure what's going on. I'll be fine once I've fallen on my face and slept for twelve hours straight."

"Of course you will be. It was rough tonight. Two died, and you ended up working on one of them."

"Don't remind me. Wouldn't have been so bad if she'd been dead when I got there, but she wasn't. And her two little kids were clinging to her, soaked in her blood and crying their eyes out. The rain would wash the blood away, but her severed artery just kept pumping it back out. I tried my best, but by the time I got there, she'd lost over half her blood. I—"

Niall reached across and gripped one of her hands. "It's all right. We can't save everybody."

"I know, but I'll see those two little girls' faces until my dying day."

Niall snaked a thread of soothing magic across the cab. At least he'd diverted her from thinking about the powerful enchantment she'd felt lurking from the sidelines. Some humans were far more susceptible to magic than others. Apparently, Meredith was one of the sensitive ones, which meant he'd either need to watch it or pair up with another of the twenty paramedics who worked the region.

In truth, he didn't need to work. He'd lived plenty long enough to have amassed a fortune, but he'd wither away from boredom with nothing to do.

He drew the van to a stop in front of her house. The door flew open, and her husband ran toward them, a frantic look on his face. She pushed the van door out of the way, jumped down, and raced into his arms. Niall caught the sound of her sobbing as he reached across the cab and pulled her door shut.

He honked once to say goodbye and backed the top-heavy vehicle into a nearby driveway. As he pulled out of the warren of streets in Meredith's housing development, his mind was a jumble. Magic had been so thick at the accident scene, he could have taken a bath in it. As it was, the ozone residue from expended power still burned his nostrils.

What the bloody fucking hell was going on?

He'd been damned careful when he selected Glenwood Springs. It was one thing to be in a huge metropolitan area with several other magic-wielders, quite another to be in a small, rural township. He'd been certain he was the only one with magic here.

Apparently, he'd been wrong.

By the time he'd returned the Medic One van to the shop and traded it for his nondescript Toyota, he had a plan. Plenty of night left, and it was still raining with no moon. He'd go home, leave the car, and shift. His jaguar senses were far more acute than his human ones, and now was the time to return to the scene—before the rain washed everything away and obliterated the scent track he hoped to find.

And follow.

Anticipation made his heart beat faster. He loved anything new. And having mysteries to solve was the absolute best.

"For Christ's sake, I need to get over myself," he muttered and reined the car back to a sedate thirty-five. For a moment there, he'd gotten up to sixty. This wasn't about him and his fascination with novelty. It was about some other paranormal beings running amok and potentially making it impossible for the rest of them to keep on flying under human radar.

The world was a much smaller place than it had been two hundred years before, and he wasn't certain where he'd go next. Maybe the Amazon jungle or a native village in some third world country. He'd be bored to tears in no time, but at least he wouldn't have a bunch of hotshots with silver-and-lead-laced bullets gunning for him.

Much like vampires, silver and lead were his undoing. They wouldn't kill him, but they'd immobilize him, so it was kind of the same thing. He parked the Toyota and hustled into his modest two-bedroom bungalow in the run-down part of town. Neighbors didn't look too closely here—at anything— and that suited him just fine. Plus, the house backed onto acres of wilderness. Perfect for his jaguar to run free.

A hooker lived across the street. A drug dealer next door. Definitely a "don't ask, don't tell" environment.

He didn't bother with the lights as he shucked his wet clothes, hanging them over anything handy. Once he was naked, he threw his magical well wide open and visualized a shadowy alley not far from the multicar pileup. He'd considered shifting and running there, but this was faster.

A muted snarl from his jaguar told him his bondmate didn't agree with his choice. The creature adored running, and they'd been in their human form for the last couple of days.

"Soon," he told it and whisked them to his selected spot. It was precisely as dark and secluded as he'd remembered. A muted gasp from behind him told him he wasn't alone, and he pivoted, night vision fully engaged. He wasn't certain quite what he'd do to the intruder, but at the very least he'd wipe any memory of what they'd seen.

A bum reeking of booze stumbled down the alleyway, breathing hard and mumbling about DTs as he put distance between himself and Niall. His head was down, and he wove from side to side. Niall hoped he didn't live to regret his choice, but he left the man to his drunken state. Clearly, hallucinations were common enough; the fellow would chalk him up to one more sensory malfunction courtesy of too much rotgut.

Before anyone else showed up, Niall summoned shift magic. The jaguar took shape with record speed amid stretching skin and reforming bones. He breathed deep, searching for clues. His cat's senses were far more acute than a human's, and the first full breath as a jaguar always rocked him with its complexity.

He drew shadows around himself and padded out of the alley, confident he was close to invisible to any passing cars. Not that he expected any at two in the morning. Or maybe it was three by now. Some of the wreckage remained. No doubt what passed for a cleanup crew here had been strained to the max to clear away what they had.

He nosed through the wrecked cars, sorting scents. Beneath the obvious stench of human distress and blood, he picked up shifter—and vampire. Not just one, either. At least three, perhaps four. A careful transit of the broken glass and twisted metal yielded wolf scent—and a big cat, but not a jaguar.

So at least two shifters had packed up with vampires. It was such an unusual association, he retraced his steps, sniffing to make certain he hadn't imagined the vamps.

At the bottom of the supernatural food chain—or the top if you were to ask them—other magic wielders avoided them like the plague. No one wanted to be associated with the undead and their taste for blood.

Niall growled low in the back of his throat. How could there be shifters here? Let alone vampires? He'd specifically checked not six months before. He dug his fangs into his lower jowl. How—or when—they'd arrived didn't matter. He wasn't asking the most important question, which was why they'd be engaging in lethal sport with humans. Even back in the Old Country, such pursuits were forbidden, with harsh punishments attached.

It was why vampires were on everyone's shit list. Their penchant for nabbing unsuspecting humans and draining them got other humans riled up. Worse, it turned people's attention to everything magical with an eye to destroying what they'd never understand.

Determined to track whoever was responsible for tonight, he sorted the strongest shifter scents leading away from the carnage and followed them, careful to cloak his presence. He didn't plan to walk into a trap. If this bunch of shifters paid no heed to the way his kin had always comported themselves, they probably ignored all the other rules too.

Like the one where shifters didn't form packs anymore.

Had the vampires snared them in some kind of enchantment? It was possible since mesmerizing prey was a vamp strategy, but since when were shifters fair game for vampires?

His magic was stronger than anything a vamp could cook up.

He settled into an easy lope following an obvious scent track. Whoever had done this hadn't believed they needed to hide their trail. Which meant they had no idea he existed.

It gave him an edge. Maybe not much of one, but he'd take anything he could get. He had a good three hours until dawn would force him back into his human body. By then, he might know something.

He hoped so. This kind of shit had to be nipped in the bud. Before humans caught on and painted targets on all their backs. If he'd been in his other form, he'd have rubbed his hands together. Nothing quite like a good scrap. Vampire blood tasted like rot and dead things, but he wouldn't let that stop him from sinking his fangs into their necks.

He couldn't kill them, but he could sure as hell slow them down.

arai Lurie kept her head down and her mouth shut. She'd gotten into this mess by being careless, letting her guard down. The only way out was to pay attention to every single detail. One of them would be her ticket to freedom.

Maybe.

If those bastard vampires pulled too many more stunts similar to the one tonight, no one like her would be safe. Humans, the canny ones, would catch on. She'd been born in the States, but she'd heard enough tales about why her kinfolk left the Old Country to understand secrecy was their greatest asset.

Even if she managed to free herself, it wouldn't mean much if humans banded together to annihilate everyone who carried a spark of magic within them.

She'd never even seen a vampire until a group of

them converged on her, her uncle, and her aunt. None of them were expecting the hostile power that had first surrounded and then immobilized them. As she thought about it, she realized the vamps must have planned and planned well. The attack occurred close to their ranch in a remote area north of Denver.

The three of them had taken a chance remaining together, but it hadn't seemed like much of one. Insofar as the few humans in the area knew, they were just one more family raising a few head of cattle and a truck garden. Her aunt and uncle had settled on the patch of land almost twenty years before when they truly had no neighbors, only open forest stretching as far as you could see.

Perfect territory for shifting.

Perfect for a quiet little abduction too. She'd tried to shift. So had Stephan and Marie, but the magical net snaring them muted their power. Her wolf had been frantic to burst free, but even adding its considerable magic didn't alter things. Marie fought back, clawing and scratching much like her mountain lion would have. One of the vamps had jumped on her and dug his incisors into her neck while Stephan writhed against another vamp's iron grip, screeching imprecations.

Maybe the vamp had misjudged with Marie. Maybe not. He'd killed her. Taken so much blood, there was no coming back. Since he hadn't even tried to turn her, Sarai was certain the death was purposeful, designed to ensure her and her uncle's cooperation.

The only things she knew about other magical creatures came from stories, but vampires could offer their wrists to the newly dead. If they fed in time, they'd join vampiric ranks as one more immortal.

The thought of her wonderful, gentle aunt as a vampire sent shivers down her back. Marie was better off well and truly dead than she would have been living on as an abomination. Tears threatened; Sarai blinked them back. She would not allow her pain to bleed through. Or her desolation.

A boot in her backside almost sent her sprawling. "Move faster," one of the three vamps who'd captured her hissed in guttural Russian-accented English.

"Leave her alone," her uncle, Stephan, tried to shove between her and the vampire.

"I'm okay," she said. Stephan had stood up to their captors with his mate lying dead in the dirt at his feet. All it earned him was a feeding session where they'd drained so much blood, she'd feared he was dead too.

Hooking an arm through Stephan's, she picked up the pace. They needed to talk. For that they needed proximity since their magic was weak. Goddess only knew how, but the vamps had figured out an enchantment that hobbled shifter power, unlocking their magical wells. Once open, the vamps plundered their power. Tonight had disgusted and horrified her. She'd done her damnedest to cut the flow of her magic, but she'd been helpless.

And now she felt drained as surely as if they'd taken her blood.

Vampires had never had this kind of power, at least according to the lore. They must have teamed up with a mage or a sorcerer. *"How are you?"* she asked Stephan in shielded telepathy she hoped wouldn't alert their vampire escort.

"Weak. Don't worry about me. Save yourself if you can." He hesitated. *"Someone must warn our kin."*

Another staunch slap across her back made her stumble. Anger boiled from her guts, and it took all her self-control not to face off with the vamp, screaming at him.

Bad idea.

They'll feed from me, and then I'll be finished. Fragile like Uncle Stephan.

"I know you're talking," the vampire who'd shoved her said. "I feel the magic." He made a grab for her arm, yanking it out from beneath Stephan's. "Twenty paces ahead."

"Go," Stephan urged.

She trotted forward. If they returned to the falling-down cabin they'd started from, they were nearly there.

Iron manacles waited, bolted to the less-rotted wall sections. No food. Very little water.

Iron.

A perfect recipe to turn her and Stephan into compliant puppets. The wolf within her growled, imploring her to fight back. She fisted both hands. She wanted to resist, but the vamps had stripped her of her weaponry.

I can't think like that. If I do, I may as well lie down and give up.

The magic surrounding her prickled unpleasantly. It felt dirty, polluted, not like any power she'd ever come across before. All the hot water in the world wouldn't clean the slime off her. Sarai shivered. Was this it? A long, slow slide that would end in her death? From Stephan's comment about saving herself, he didn't expect to make it out of their predicament alive.

None of their family was close enough to help, even if she had a way of reaching them. When they'd first come to the States, shifters made the decision to spread out. Her parents were on the West Coast near Los Angeles. Her brothers and sisters scattered all over the place. Stephan and Marie hadn't had any children of their own, which was part of the reason they'd been delighted when she'd moved in with them.

Her mind was rambling. She should be focused on escape, not a rehash of Lurie family history. The nasty magic poked her in the side. She understood well enough and stepped off the dirt road and onto the path leading to the cabin. How had the vamps even found it? Mostly buried in deadfall, blackened foliage suggested they'd had to burn a path to the fallen-in front door.

It reminded her of a crypt, which might be what had drawn her undead captors. She glanced at the sky. Daybreak was close. At least she and Stephan got a break while the vamps huddled in the underground portion of the cabin—the part built into a substantial hill.

If only they went to sleep in coffins or something, but they were very much awake. Far as she could tell, they never slept. Or ate.

It gave her an idea. "Hey." She aimed her voice at the nearest vamp. It didn't even turn around. She swallowed around dry places in her throat. "If you don't feed us and give us water, there'll be no more magic for you to steal."

The vampire did turn then. Dark hair streamed down his shoulders, and he skewered her with midnight-blue eyes. Dressed in jeans, boots, and a leather jacket, he could have passed for an extra in a Hollywood Western.

All three of the undead held an unholy beauty. She'd learned not to look too closely at them because their appearance drew her, made her long to present her neck for their fangs. Normally, her own magic would have protected her from self-destructive impulses, but she no longer had access to her power. She felt it swimming within her, but it may as well have lived ten miles away for all the good it did.

The vamp shrugged and turned well-formed, long-fingered hands palms up. "No food here."

"Tell me something I don't know." Sarai forged ahead. Not much to lose. "I have no idea what kind of plans you have for us tonight, but if you don't provide fuel for our bodies, our magic will wither along with our physical abilities."

The vamp barked something in his language with its guttural intonation that reminded her of Russian with extra, out-of-control consonants. Another vamp glanced his way and replied.

A sharp tug in her midsection hurt so much, she folded her arms over her stomach, trying not to cry out. Magic—her magic—flowed to the vampires, except her reservoir was sucking fumes. Must be why it felt like she'd just been fileted with a dull knife.

The sounds of small rodents reached her sensitive hearing. Even before she saw them, she recognized what the vampire had done. He'd twisted her power into a malevolent version of the Pied Piper of Hamelin to draw game. As soon as the cavalcade of rabbits, rats, mice, and raccoons drew near, he grabbed them one by one, passing them to his undead buddies to drain.

Sarai looked on, horrified. It was a perversion of their magic to use it to lure innocents.

"Different rule book," her wolf spoke up. *"Don't think about it. Eat."*

It was good advice, but her stomach turned over. She hoped the meat would stay down. "We need a fire," she said in a voice she barely recognized.

"Not going to happen." The vampire who'd noted there wasn't any food looked up from a large brown rabbit. "Figure things out."

Stephan grabbed a rat from the quickly growing pile of dead bodies. Pushing revulsion to a distant back burner, Sarai did the same. She tugged a small blade from a thigh sheath. The vamps had found it, determined it didn't pose a threat to them, and let her keep it.

"Water?" Stephan croaked as he used his own knife to skin the rat.

"You are more trouble than you're worth." The third vampire set his perfect mouth is a harsh line but ducked into the cabin, returning with a filthy, cracked glass carafe.

"I'll fill it," Sarai said. "Extend your hold on me so I can go as far as the stream behind the cabin."

The vampire narrowed dark eyes, muttered, "I think not," and headed in the direction of the creek.

"Wash the dirt out of it," she yelled after him and was met with hoots and jeers from the other two. Blood ran down their chins, giving them a ghoulish appearance.

She went back to the rat. As soon as she had the skin off it and the gut sack out, she chewed meat from the bones. It was bitter but not nearly as horrible as she'd imagined it would be. She laid the bones aside and grabbed another one.

The vampire returned and dropped the water jug between her and Stephan. She handed it to her uncle. He was in worse shape than she was. He drank, throat working, and she noted he'd finished his rat off too.

"We need to move this party inside," the vamp with the blue eyes said and gathered the dead animals into his arms.

Soiled magic—the sick combination of vampire and mage or whatever they'd joined with to augment their power—prodded her unpleasantly, and she snapped up the second rat and the water, ducking to get inside the cabin. Time for her next request. "We still require food." She tilted her chin at a defiant angle. "If you chain us to the wall, we won't be able to eat or drink. By the time today is done, we'll be too weak for you to use for anything."

Harsh language flew fast and furious as the vampires argued about her statement. It happened to be true, which might push them in the direction she hoped. She debated saying more but didn't want to appear too eager. Normal vamps were weaker in daylight.

Her plan wasn't elegant, but if she and Stephan weren't shackled, maybe they could push against their magical bonds enough to make it out the door. The cabin was small, maybe only fifteen feet square, and the vampires would be in the back section, the one dug into the hill. Once outside, the vampires would be slow, clumsy, even with the infusion of whatever was fueling their unnatural ability—beyond her and Stephan's power.

Outside in daylight was the key.

She tried again to solve the puzzle of what was going on and came up empty-handed. Some other source of magic had to be in play. Normally, vampires wouldn't be able to capture shifters. Yet they'd not only kidnapped her family, they'd siphoned power from them.

Sarai cleared her head of everything but the moment. She'd only get one chance. Even though she didn't understand the vamps' language, they had to be debating if they could trust her and her uncle. Not wanting to appear too invested, she pulled out her knife again and went to work on the rat, repeating her actions from earlier. This one was female and pregnant. Sarai dropped the fetal sac atop the gut sack and ate the rat anyway. Her wolf wouldn't have wasted a second feeling sorry for the baby rats that would never be, and neither would she.

Stephan was eating too, as if he didn't have a care in the world. He'd moved on to a marmot. Bigger and fattier than rats, it looked good. She drank some water and held out a hand for a chunk of marmot. Stephan gave it to her, an unreadable expression on his face.

She felt for him. Marie had been the center of his universe. To leave her without even a decent burial must be killing him. Shifters burned their dead. It freed the bond animal to move on. So not only was Marie dead, her mountain lion was trapped in limbo. No longer part of this world but unable to return to the animals' special place.

Anger twisted her stomach into a knot. She sent calming thoughts inward. No point throwing up nutrition she needed. She could think about all this at the other end of it. Right now, she had to be very present. Looking back—or too far forward—was counterproductive.

The vamp conversation died away, and the blue-eyed one glared at her and Stephan. "Today, we leave you unshackled. But we will be watching. One false move, and you both die."

The dark-eyed vampire cackled. "Now that we know how easy you are to capture, we don't need you."

"Ha! We never needed them," the third vampire cut in. "They were our experiment. One that worked, I might add."

"Silence." The first vampire made a chopping motion and retreated to the back wall of the cabin, squatting as he leaned against one wall. Blood smears from the animals he'd drained dotted his chin and jacket.

Sarai avoided looking at him. Would him having a belly full of blood make a difference? Were vamps who'd fed slower, more tractable? Stephan poked her and handed her another chunk of marmot. She chewed and swallowed mechanically, waiting for time to elapse.

What were the vampires up to? It couldn't only be these three. Had they formed some kind of consortium with plans to crawl to the top of the magical heap? The idea was so ludicrous, she almost choked on the marmot. Vampires were ancient and a scourge, but no way could they take on all the magic-wielders living in North America, even if they sacrificed humans as collateral damage.

Enough people had watched *Supernatural* and

some of the other paranormal television shows and movies to arm themselves with iron sabers and lop off heads right and left. For one exhilarating moment, she hoped it would happen. Hoped every single vampire would die a hideous death, never to be reborn as anything.

"Listen up," her wolf said. *"You can't talk with Stephan, but I have no problem conversing with his bond animal."*

The implication hit her with all the subtlety of a runaway train. She muffled the gasp that wanted out, intent on not alerting the vampires anything had changed.

She had a way to talk with her uncle. Finally. To make certain, she cast a surreptitious glance toward the vampires' part of the cabin. All three of them hunkered, looking like crows perched on a telephone line. None of them so much as looked up. Was her theory about feeding making them sluggish more than a lucky guess?

Stephan carved off more marmot, a benign expression on his face. Like many shifters, he didn't age, and his hair was the same golden color it had been for his two hundred plus years. Blue eyes, an unlined face, and a powerful build paired with a kind and generous disposition.

"Tell his cat I love him."

"He already knows," the wolf retorted. *"Stephan says this is your chance to escape. Once you're outside, run like the wind. When we're beyond the perimeter of their spell, we'll shift and run even harder."*

She smothered excitement in case the vampires were keyed into her heartrate or blood pressure.

"Stephan isn't coming," her wolf went on. *Them feeding from him means he won't be nimble enough. He will only slow you down."*

"I'm not going without him." Stubborn, protective, she drew a line in the sand.

"He says you must. You're the only hope for our kind. Don't you see, we have to warn everyone. Had we been warded, they wouldn't have captured us."

Sarai wasn't so sure about that. Warding might have slowed the vamps down, though, allowed her and her family to shift. Her power was returning slowly, courtesy of raw meat and water. She judged the distance to the door. Roughly five feet separated her from its gaping maw.

She slitted her eyes, switching to her psychic view and hoping it wouldn't alert the vampires she was up to something. Ley lines shimmered into view along with the black ropes of foul magic looped around her and her uncle. The rope was loose, but she bet it could tighten in the blink of an eye. If she timed it, leapt just right, she could avoid the rope snapping shut around her.

Sarai's heart thudded. No slowing it down this time. She was going to do this. There'd never be a better time.

Unfamiliar magic blasted through the broken door, and a tall, broad man, naked body slabbed with muscle burst inside, an iron saber swinging. Dark hair fell straight as a stick past his shoulders, and his silver eyes blazed hot with fury. He avoided the rope so neatly, he must have seen it too and charged the vampires struggling to their feet. One swipe cleaved through bone and sinew, beheading the lead vampire.

"Come on!" Sarai shrieked to Stephan. Grabbing his arm, she dragged him through the door and out into weak daylight.

Nothing stood in their way, and they ran back to the road and then in the opposite direction from where they'd come. Sarai's sides heaved. Sweat slicked her entire body, but she kept going.

"Shift!" Stephan yelled. The air around him liquified and glistened until a golden mountain lion stood in the midst of a pile of torn clothing.

Sarai didn't hesitate. She gave her wolf its head. Together with Stephan's bondmate, they left the road, hustling deeper into the forest. Now was a time to lose themselves. They'd figure everything else out later, after they'd made their way back to the ranch and Marie's body.

Who had saved them? Another shifter, but one whose power wasn't affected by the vampires' poison. Maybe because the stranger had grabbed the upper hand before the vampires had a chance to get their claws into him. Her wolf's tongue lolled. Unexpected freedom gave her hope there was a way to counteract the impossible after all.

"We need to find him. Thank him." Stephan's gruff voice rolled through her mind.

"We will. As soon as we honor our dead."

"I am still weak, niece. We must hunt before I have the strength to return to my fallen mate."

Sarai understood. She wasn't at her best, either. Two dead rats and a few bits of marmot were all she'd had to eat in two days. *"First game I see will be ours,"* she assured her uncle. He'd taken her in after her parents banished her. It was the least she could do.

CHAPTER 3

A few hours earlier

Solidly entrenched in the scent trail that was doing nothing but growing stronger, Niall didn't realize how close he was to his target until it was almost too late to avoid discovery. He slowed, careful to maintain absolute silence. If he remembered right, vampire hearing was nearly as acute as his own.

Rage had run hot once he understood vampires imprisoned two shifters, and anger always undermined his judgment.

Why weren't the shifters fighting back? They were docile, almost as if the vamps had mesmerized them. He wasn't near enough to sort out the fine points, but any shifter worth his magic should be immune to vampire mind control.

He dropped back until he was certain he wouldn't be noticed. Once the group ahead of him—three vampires and two captive shifters—turned off onto a little-used side trail, he stopped and ran options through his mind.

If he could count on help from the wolf and mountain lion shifters, he'd charge the vamps. Problem was, he wasn't certain the shifters would lift a paw to help him. If they were sunk far enough in the vampires' foul spell, they might attack him right along with the vamps.

No. Moving forward as a jaguar was off the table. What he needed was an iron blade. Then he could return in his human body and behead these three monstrosities. He wasn't at all sure what to do with the shifters once they were free, but he'd cross that street when he got there.

The wolf shifter was female and might have been striking if it weren't for her slumped shoulders and straggly red hair that hadn't been washed in days. She was tall like the mountain lion shifter, but slender, and her posture screamed defeat. It was a guess on Niall's part, but the cat shifter smelled like a relative. Nothing so close as a parent, but perhaps an uncle or cousin.

Why hadn't the mountain lion protected his kinswoman? Niall gritted his teeth in frustration. The tableau playing out in front of him would never have happened on his watch.

He backtracked a good half mile before summoning shift magic. Dawn was breaking. That little item would work in his favor. Vampires couldn't tolerate daylight, which meant they'd gone to ground somewhere along that overgrown trail. Niall voted for a cave—these mountains were riddled with old mineshafts—or an abandoned hut.

Shit! The shifters had looked like little better than minions. How could any of his kinfolk, however distant, allow themselves to end up slaves to evil? Wickedness that had pulled the linchpin causing tonight's deadly accident. Shifters were better than that. Vampires weren't, but working on their own, they didn't possess sufficient magic to craft the mysterious fog that triggered the crash.

He had a lot of unanswered questions. Anchored in his human body, he visualized his home and whisked himself there to collect an antique saber. When he'd decided he couldn't part with a few of his treasures, collected over his long lifetime, he'd had no idea he'd actually need any of them. Crouching in front of the bedroom closet, he reached through magical shrouding and withdrew leather riddled with mouse toothmarks, unfolding it reverently.

Three long blades, a fencing foil, two hunting

knives, and an oaken case containing jewelry that had been in his family for decades came into view. He selected the heaviest blade and wrapped everything else back up, placing it behind the enchantment designed to skewer anyone who dared disturb his cache.

He really should give the jewelry to some other family member, one more likely to pick a mate, but that was a problem for another day. He started to dress but thought better of it. Clothes would be an impediment if he had to shift, and he had no bloody idea what the two shifters would do once the vampires had been beheaded.

If they took their animal forms intent on fighting him, he'd have no choice but to transform into a jaguar. He hoped it wouldn't come to that, hoped he'd be able to undo whatever spell held them captive. Assuming he was able to counteract the curse that had turned them into senseless minions, he'd give them a solid piece of his mind.

It was unthinkable they'd allowed themselves to be seized in the first place. Had his kind grown feeble? Lazy? It had been years since he'd spent any time around other shifters, so he had no way of knowing.

A quick glance outside told him daylight was firmly established. At least it had stopped raining. Time to go. Opening himself to magic, he let it sweep through him as he returned to the spot half a mile from his quarry. He didn't hesitate. No need for stealth now.

The vampires were trapped wherever they'd chosen for their lair. Bloodlust ran hot, and he hurried, engaging his psychic view after he left the dirt road for the winding track through thick timber. Branches crackled beneath his feet, but he didn't waste time trying to be mitigate the signs of his approach.

The shifters should hear him. Maybe. From the looks of things earlier, they were so depleted they might not sense him moving toward them. He ducked and wove, avoiding overhanging branches and deadfall blocking what had never been a very well-made trail.

Any other time, he'd have enjoyed the rich pine scents and the springy loam underfoot. Shifters had an affinity for the natural world, as opposed to vampires who did their damnedest to destroy it. The trick they'd played tonight was typical vampire hooliganry. They didn't see it as criminal. In their warped minds, killing was fun.

Niall bet the reason their distinctive stench had permeated the scene was because they'd snuck around draining who they could. Anger twisted his guts into a knot. He kept returning to the same place. Vampires were dicks, but shifter magic enabled them to execute tonight's crime. He shut down that line of thought. He needed a cool head right now, and single-minded focus.

Vampires, not shifters. He'd deal with the wolf and cat later.

A ramshackle cabin came into view. Almost buried by deadfall, someone had burned a path through it and not too long ago judging by how fresh the tree scars and charred marks were. Odd the shifters hadn't come outside. Surely, they sensed him.

Niall bolted through the channel of trees canting at crazy angles and ducked to enter the falling-down cabin. As he'd expected, the vampires were gathered as far from the entrance as they could get. Even better, they were sluggish to respond.

The wolf shifter cast a startled glance his way out of very blue eyes, but Niall ignored her and headed straight for the three vamps who were struggling to their feet. Not caring about a fair fight—there was no such thing where vamps were concerned—he swung the blade, enjoying the crunch as it cleaved flesh, sinew, and bone.

The vampire's head rolled from his body, followed by a torrent of black ichor. Depending how old the abomination was, he'd deteriorate into nothing more than bones damned fast.

Behind him, the wolf shifter screeched, "Come on!" The sounds of her and her companion exiting the cabin heartened Niall. At least they had some spirit left. He could find them later. Now was the time to finish what he'd begun. One of the vampires grabbed his sword arm and sank his teeth into Niall's forearm.

Niall pivoted, switched the blade to his other hand and sliced it neatly through the vampire's bent neck. This time, black blood sprayed him, smarting wherever it landed. He'd have burns, but they were nothing, a small price to pay for the pleasure of ridding the world of vampires.

The vampire's body crumpled to the dirt floor, but its head was still attached to Niall's arm, and its ungodly blue eyes glared at him.

"Really?" Niall moved to Gaelic, stringing curses atop more curses as he flung his arm against a wall. The vampire's skull cracked open like an overripe melon, spilling red-and-black goo in its wake. The jaws opened, and Niall shook himself free of the head.

The last vampire had scooted as far from Niall as he could get and remain next to the cabin's rear wall. He extended his hands. "I surrender."

Niall choked back laughter. "Really? I wasn't aware your kind knew what the word meant."

The vamp looked away, clearly past trying anything as shoddy as mind-control games. He'd figured out Niall wasn't a chump who'd fall for such things.

"Go ahead. Make all the fun of me you want, but let me go."

"I suppose you'll promise to behave yourself forever, right?" Niall mocked. He loved having the upper hand, and there was no way the vampire was going to get away from him.

Both of them knew it.

He narrowed his eyes. "I propose a trade."

"What kind of trade?" The vampire made a show of jauntiness, but his eyes flickered with uncertainty.

"How did you force the shifters to open their magic to you?"

"You'd like to know, wouldn't you?"

Niall nodded. "It's the price of that freedom you want so badly."

A combination snort and grunt rolled from the vampire, and he pushed upright, facing Niall. A fey light displaced the defeat in his eyes as he squared his shoulders. "My life is forfeit no matter what I do. You can kill me. If you don't, I'll walk past you out into the day, and it will finish the job. Your choice, *shifter.*"

The way he said shifter sounded like the worst kind of curse. Niall hefted the blade and swung a third time. This one's neck was harder to cleave, which meant he was younger. The other two were smoking, stinking piles of bones. It might take months before this one was quite as decomposed. He stepped out of the way but wasn't fast enough, and still more black blood coated him. It stank of rot and dead things lying too long beneath a hot sun.

Niall employed magic to gather what he could in the way of clues. Ropes of dark magic were unraveling fast in the area the shifters had been. It explained how the vampires had held them, but not how they'd tapped into their magic. What had the vampire said? His life was forfeit no matter what choice he made.

Did that mean someone else was involved in kidnapping the shifters?

He inhaled deeply, seeking clues, but all he smelled was vampire. The sound of a nearby creek drew him outside, and he trudged around the cabin to where water flowed down a tight ravine full of tangled brush. Kneeling, he washed his blade, setting it aside to dry before he stood in the creek and sluiced his body with icy water until no trace of black blood remained.

He still smelled vampire, but with three dead ones not ten feet away, it wasn't surprising. Picking up his blade, he returned to the cabin door still intent on making certain he didn't miss something critical. Something that might help unravel how two shifters ended up captives.

"Give me a chance," the jaguar demanded.

Niall was getting nowhere, and he didn't have any better ideas, so he laid the saber aside and ceded their form to his cat. Amid whisker rustling, sneezing, and snuffling, the jaguar padded inside the cabin, making a thorough transit before trotting back outside.

"Whew. Stinks in there."

Niall knew exactly how bad it smelled. *"Did you find anything?"* he asked.

"Maybe. I don't want to influence you, but take your form back and check for mage energy."

Back in his human form, Niall whistled long and low. Mage energy? If his bondmate was right and vampires had joined forces with mages, it was a disaster in the making.

He took a deep breath, all the way to the bottom of his lungs, blew it out, and did it again to clear his churning mind. Eyes closed, enhanced senses on full alert, he hunted for the telltale ping of mage energy. High and bright, nothing else in the magical realm felt quite like it.

A flare of magic that shouldn't have been there teased him. He moved toward it, back inside the falling-down hut, and kept his nose close to floor level where the enchantment was strongest. Made sense if it helped trap the shifters. After he'd covered the dirt-floored hovel from front to back and side to side, he returned outside.

"Well?" the jaguar demanded.

"I believe you're correct." Niall adopted a formal

tone. "If you are, it means we're headed back into the thick of an old war."

"*I remember. I was there,*" the cat reminded him. "*Right along with you.*"

Niall snatched up the blade. He needed to find the wolf and cat shifters, but first he needed to think. He balanced on the balls of his feet, impervious to small rocks beneath him or the chill wind blowing on his still-wet skin.

Mages were failed shifters. Those whose magic didn't run quite straight enough to attract a bondmate. None of them accepted their second-class status, though. They all did everything they could before the truth they'd never be bonded sank in. By then, they were hostile, bitter, and filled with hatred for every shifter with a bond animal.

The last mage-shifter war had played itself out in the middle of the seventeen hundreds. It hadn't been pretty. There'd been so much carnage on both sides the sorcerers' council, concerned by the rising death toll, decreed an end to the fighting.

Niall pounded a fist into a nearby tree. He'd thought their internecine squabbles had been private, but apparently vampires had discovered them. In true vampire form, they'd found a way to leverage hatred to their benefit.

If mages willingly lent their power to vampires, it

would make vamps strong enough to capture shifters, and a whole lot of other magic-wielders too.

It meant shifters weren't safe from their magic being diverted and turned to dark purposes. Maybe the pair who'd fled weren't as lackluster as Niall had judged them. Perhaps they'd been assailed by magic so pervasive they'd had no choice. Formulae existed that assessed additive magics and what the net result would be, except he'd never been much for burying himself in books.

Someone had their ancient lore tomes, but he had no idea who.

He stood in the clearing, sword in hand, the stench of vampire hideously strong, and plotted a short-term game plan. He needed to sound the alarm to all his kin, a process he could begin via telepathy. Before he did that, he should catch up with the wolf and the cat. Maybe they'd have critical information, material he needed. No point in disseminating one message to shifters near enough to reach with magic only to end up countermanding it with a second one.

Things would be bad enough once this news got out. Some shifters would probably want to fight, but that would bring their supernatural identities into the light of day. Niall had enjoyed the last two hundred years where he wasn't constantly looking over his shoulder for the hangman waiting to drape a noose around his neck.

He wasn't anxious to trade his peace of mind for the furtive existence that had driven him out of Ireland.

"Yeah, that peace of mind went up in smoke when I scented shifter and vampire at the accident."

"Good thing you said it," the jaguar noted. *"Otherwise I would have."*

Niall glanced skyward. The sun was squarely above him. Half the day was gone. He was due at work tonight, which meant he had to get moving. He tracked the shifters to where they'd taken their animal forms, and then he stopped. He should return the blade to his home, but he didn't want to take the time.

He raised his head, scenting the air. The wolf and cat had headed into the forest, leaving the road behind. He picked his way after them until he found a cairn of standing stones. It was a perfect place to leave the saber, and he tucked it between two boulders, shrouding its hiding place with a magical overlay.

No longer burdened by needing hands to carry the blade, he let the shift magic take him. Four legs with substantial claws were far better than two for negotiating the rough terrain. An hour passed before he closed the distance between himself and the two shifters. They crouched over a smallish deer they'd just killed. A creek burbled past nearby.

Niall released the enchantment keeping his magic hidden.

The wolf let go of her hold on the deer and whipped to face him, golden eyes narrowed in challenge. The mountain lion was a little slower, but he too spun to face Niall, growling a challenge.

"*I rescued you,*" Niall said, and then shifted amid a bright flare of power.

The mountain lion bowed his head. Magic shimmered around the wolf as she reclaimed her human form. Blood streaked her cheeks and chin. She tried to wipe it away, but all it did was smear.

Niall stared at high, firm breasts, a delicate waist, and flared hips. Red hair trailed almost to knee level, and her eyes were a clear, perfect blue. He'd bet his last spell she had an ass to die for. Heat licked at his loins, desperate, primitive. He'd just come from a battlefield. Warriors often traded swords for fucking. It reminded them how precious life was.

"Thank you for your timely intervention." The wolf's voice was low and sweet. It forced his overheated gaze away from her body. He was behaving abysmally, like a boor.

"Indeed, many thanks from me also." The

mountain cat was human as well. "My name is Stephan Lurie. Sarai is my niece."

"I'm Niall MacLier, and I figured you were related," he stammered, feeling like a fool. A familiar fullness between his legs told him he had to be sporting a full-blown erection. Embarrassment didn't make a dent in his lust. He needed to get laid more, but he couldn't fix that problem anytime soon.

Maybe not at all the way things were going.

He cleared his throat. "I finished off the vampires, but I need to know how they bent you to their will."

Stephan nodded, a somber expression on his face. "We should have known better, but we've lived for years at our ranch without any problems. We grew careless."

"I disagree," Sarai broke in. "We've never had any need to ward ourselves, so I fail to see how not taking a precaution we've never needed before can be labeled careless."

Niall buried a grin. He liked Sarai. She had spunk. Probably meant she'd be a hellion in bed. His groin throbbed, and he shut down the sexual imagery.

"All right." Niall was still on a fact-gathering mission. "You weren't warded. Then what happened?"

"Those three vampires came out of nowhere, but it wasn't just vampire magic," Stephan said. "I felt something else."

"We thought maybe mages were behind this," Sarai said. Her eyes sheened. "My aunt Marie was with us. They killed her."

"Goddess be damned, that's terrible." Niall's arousal vanished in the face of Sarai's grief.

"We must return. Offer her proper rites so her animal may run free again." Stephan spoke stiffly, as if the words cost him.

"Of course. Would you like my help?" Niall asked.

"If it's freely offered," Stephan replied.

"It is," Niall assured him.

"We must warn everyone we can," Sarai spoke up.

"I've already begun, but telepathy only goes so far," Stephan said.

"I'll see what I can do to extend our reach," Niall reassured them. "Where is Marie?" An image skimmed across his mind. "It's enough. I can find her."

Stephan wrapped a hand around Sarai's arm. "Come, child. We will take a chance no one sees us."

"If we come out inside the house, they won't." Sarai sounded fierce.

Alarms sounded in Niall's mind. Inside a house would appeal to vampires since it was daytime. "Hang on. If vampires located you once, they can find you again. By now, they all know three of their legion are dead."

"I refuse to leave my mate in her current state." Stephan stood tall. "Maybe I should go alone."

"Wait here," Niall said. "I left the blade so I could shift. I'm going to retrieve it, and then we'll all go. At least that way if we head straight into an ambush, we'll have something to even the score."

"I like the way you think, son." Stephan held out a hand, and Niall shook it.

"I'd watch it with the *son* jargon. I'm probably older than you."

"We can figure that out once Marie's soul is on its way to the afterlife. And her bondmate is free."

"Don't think a thing about it," Sarai said. "I'm past fifty human years, and he still calls me child."

"It's because you are a child to me..."

Their good-natured banter continued to flow as Niall summoned magic to return him to where he'd hidden the saber. Stephan was a decent man, and Sarai stunning to the nth power, but she wasn't for him.

She needed a man who was mate material, something he'd never been. Women were a diversion to him, a pleasant one, but nothing more.

"Aye, mate, keep telling yourself that," he muttered as the stones hiding the sword formed in front of him. He was still giving himself advice when he headed back to the clearing where he'd left the two shifters.

He'd never paid much attention to behaving

honorably where women were concerned, but this time would be different. He'd see to it.

If he didn't, he had a feeling Stephan would do it for him. The man was fond of his niece and defensive as a cat on the prowl. Besides, there was something familiar about the cat shifter. Niall might have known him a long time back, but he couldn't quite draw the memory out of its hidey hole.

CHAPTER 4

Sarai bent and rinsed her face and hands in the creek. The blood had already dried, but she did the best she could and looked longingly at the deer carcass. The animal had been young, tender, and a big step up from eating raw rats and marmots.

Stephan growled, and her head snapped up. "What? It's a shame to let that food go to waste."

Her uncle walked close and directed his words into her ear. "You stay away."

"But we were just eating it," she protested.

"Not what I meant." Stephan exhaled sharply. "We don't have much time before Niall returns, but I saw how he looked at you—"

"Uncle. He rescued us."

"I'm well aware of that fact, but that one like as not has women in every town, lots of them. He probably hasn't changed at all since our boat of shifters landed in New York." Stephan made a face. "Damn if he didn't spend the six weeks we were at sea moving from one bed to the next."

Sarai resisted a strong temptation to roll her eyes. Stephan had always been an overprotective papa bear type, but this was ridiculous.

"I only just met him." She turned a disappointed look her uncle's way. "We have bigger problems. I'm not exactly in a mating mood."

"He can be quite persuasive. Watch yourself."

"Hush. He'll be back soon."

Magic flared, making her words prophetic as Niall strode toward them, blade in hand.

"Handy implement." Stephan's voice was gruff. "Where'd you come by it?"

Niall shrugged. "I brought it from Ireland, along with a few other relics I couldn't bear to part with. It's been sitting in the bottom of one closet or another since our ship landed. You were on my ship, right? You look familiar."

"Yup. I was on it." Stephan's words skirted rebuke but didn't quite get there.

"Thought so. I never forget a face…"

Sarai took advantage of the men's conversation to take a good, hard look at Niall. He was a hell of an attractive man. Thick, black hair framed a high forehead and squared off chin dotted with a couple of day's beard growth. His eyes had blazed silver in the cabin, but that was because he was partially immersed in his animal nature. Now they shaded to a deep, rich brown. He was tall, with muscles bunching along his shoulders and back and down his arms. Legs like small tree trunks supported him, and between them his cock had deflated somewhat.

She'd noticed it in full bloom. How could she not? Long, thick, and proud, it had jutted from his body. Despite her words about not being in a mating mood, her nether regions twitched. She hadn't had a man in years. Between her uncle's eagle eye and her aunt's nattering about saving herself for just the right mate, she'd had to sneak around to have any kind of a sex life. Aside from a few spontaneous tumbles in the small back room of her shop, she'd lived like a nun.

She had a feeling Niall would more than make up for her long stint being celibate. Maybe him being a womanizer was a good thing. She wouldn't have to worry about any hard-to-extricate-herself-from entanglements. Truth was, she loved her freedom. Marie had paraded dozens of potential mates through their home, and Sarai had found something wrong with every single one.

Her aunt finally took the hint, and the cavalcade of shifters in search of a mate had first slowed and then faded entirely, leaving her free to concentrate on her psychic shop in one of Denver's poorer sections. Over time, she'd built a decent business constructing astrological charts, casting tarot spreads, and matching up crystals with people's energies.

Niall was a Gemini. She was certain of it. His energy had that barely suppressed passion characteristic of the mutable air sign. She itched for details to corroborate her impressions, and maybe she'd get them. Later.

An image of his cock, sticking straight out from the mat of black curls between his legs tantalized her, and she pressed her thighs together. She was Cancer to the core, an almost perfect mate for don't-tie-me-down Gemini—

"Niece!" Stephan's command cut through her musings.

"Yes?" She focused on her uncle.

"We're ready to depart."

She walked close to where the men stood on the far side of the deer, understanding this would be a group teleport so they'd all come out in the same spot.

"Open your magic to me," Stephan commanded. "I will control the casting."

She expected Niall to protest, assume the alpha position, but he remained relaxed, ready, with an unreadable expression on his face. What had he and her uncle talked about after she'd stopped listening? She cringed inwardly and hoped Stephan hadn't threatened Niall with mayhem if he so much as looked cross-eyed at her.

She hadn't realized it until that moment, but she wanted to get to know the jaguar shifter better. A whole lot better. So what if it wasn't permanent?

Magic settled around her, drawing her out of her thoughts, all of which pointed to Niall. The wooded glen fell away, replaced by the familiar walls of the farmhouse. A place that still smelled of her aunt. Sadness welled, superseding her earlier reflections.

Niall and Stephan exchanged a pointed glance before fanning out in different directions. Sarai scented the air. Had vampires invaded their home? It didn't appear so. No one seemed to need her, so she darted into her room and tossed on an old set of sweats, followed by socks and boots.

"Out here!" Niall's voice rang from the direction of the back porch.

She headed toward him at a dead run, not knowing what she'd find.

Stephan was already there when she arrived, anger kindling in his eyes. "You're right. Goddammit. They were here and not that long ago."

"Let's retrieve Marie before they desecrate her

further." Niall's grim expression could have been carved in stone.

He was still naked. Still gorgeous, but Sarai wasn't paying attention. With the men behind her, she sprinted to where her aunt had fallen. It was a good quarter mile, and she was breathing hard when she fell to her knees next to her aunt's body. It was totally drained of blood, but that had happened before they were herded away from their home.

Offered no choice but to follow the vampires.

She gathered Marie into her arms, heart aching for the cat shifter who'd been her aunt. Marie was a gentle, giving soul who'd loved unstintingly. Grief cut deep, and tears tracked down her face.

Stephan knelt next to her, holding his arms out for his mate. Sarai kissed Marie's white forehead and gave her to Stephan, who rose to his feet with Marie clasped against his chest.

"Where do you wish to consecrate her?" Niall asked.

"Near her home. It's what she would have wanted," Stephan replied. His features twisted in sorrow, but he remained stoic.

Sarai followed the men back to the farmhouse. She bore witness as they summoned mage fire to cremate Marie. Fueled by strong magic, the flames burned her to nothing but bones and ash in a matter of minutes.

Her bondmate formed above the funeral pyre, head bowed in sorrow as it, too, bid Marie farewell.

"Come with me." Stephan motioned to Niall once the fire had died to ashes. "My clothes should fit you, and then we'll move forward."

Niall shook his head. "I have to get home. I'm late for work as it is."

"Is your work more important than saving our people?" Stephan's question was quiet, without inflection, but he turned his unrelenting gaze on Niall. Sarai knew that look since she'd been its beneficiary on many occasions. It wasn't the kind of skewering you could squirm out from under.

She transferred her full attention to Niall. How would he respond? Would he tell her uncle he'd take care of things from his end as best he could and be done with it?

Her eyes widened. If he did that, it might mean she never saw him again.

Back off, sweetie. Her inner voice was tart. *Focus on what's important.*

Niall set his mouth in a determined line, but it didn't make his lips any less kissable. "What'd you have in mind?" he asked Stephan.

Her uncle nodded. "That's better. Surely you recall our last war with the mages?" At Niall's nod, he went on. "We can't afford another like it. Not in the modern world. Humans would decide all of us were a threat, and they have far more effective methods of tracking and killing than they possessed in the Old Country."

"I already figured out that part," Niall said dryly. "Once humans discover us, we're all fair game. They won't discriminate between mages or shifters or even vampires."

"Maybe we could teach them," Sarai spoke up. Both men turned disapproving glances her way, and she shrugged. "Men aren't as intolerant as they were in the world you were born into. Or as superstitious. They don't view supernatural phenomena as something that has to be eradicated—"

"Your experiences don't exactly bear that out." Stephan's words held a sharp edge that shut her up fast.

Niall made a chopping motion. "Och, darling. Sure and you've been brainwashed by the media."

"Watch the endearments," Stephan snarled. "She's my family."

Niall rolled his eyes. "Pay attention to the important parts, mate. Do you disagree with me? Or do you believe humankind have embraced diversity, like your local Internet provider would like you to think?"

"What I believe isn't important," he retorted. "What comes next is. We must warn our kin, convene a council meeting, and pick a direction most of us agree with."

"The council's been defunct since we set foot in North America," Niall muttered.

"We'll form a new one." Stephan shut his jaw with an audible *clack*. "Will you work with me, or is that job of yours more important?"

Color spread from Niall's chest upward, reddening his skin. He was angry. Stephan had that effect on people with his cut-to-the-chase way of addressing issues.

Sarai tried out various placating statements, a skill she'd learned from Marie, but none of them fit. They were at a crossroads, and if they didn't fight back, the combination of mage and vampire power could be their undoing.

Perhaps.

She wasn't as certain as her uncle and Niall that humans couldn't be reasoned with. The ones who patronized her shop were charmed by the unseen world. Whether their fascination extended to the reality of her being able to shift into a wolf was a huge unknown. When she'd taken a chance and revealed herself to humans thirty-five years ago, it had gone so badly, her parents exiled her.

That was how she'd ended up with Stephan and Marie.

Niall raked his hands through his hair, making muscles ripple through his chest and upper arms. Sarai tried not to look, but it was a losing battle. The man oozed come-fuck-me vibes. She bet he didn't spend too many nights alone, and the thought made her come alive with hunger.

Is that what was wrong with all the men Marie marched through here? I found them too tame for my taste?

"Let me do this," Niall was saying. "I'll teleport home, dress, and get my car. I do want to stop by the paramedic office and let them know I have to take some time off. A family emergency in Ireland might buy me enough time." He paused long enough to take a measured breath. "I've learned not to burn my bridges. I like being an EMT, and if I stay in this region, they're the only employer."

Sarai's ears perked up. Emergency medicine was a perfect Gemini vocation with a constantly changing backdrop of crises. "When's your birthday?" she blurted, and then shook her head. "Sorry, I have no idea where that came from."

"I do," her uncle said sourly. "It's that psychic shop of yours. You got taken in by your own line of bullshit with charts and tarot and whatever else you do down there."

She bristled and stood straighter. "Women work

now. It isn't like it used to be where my mother did the same things I do, but for free. I like what I do. There's truth in my charts—and my readings. I have customers who come back over and over." Her tone grew more pointed. "They don't consider what I do *bullshit*."

"Neither do I," Niall cut in smoothly, in pure Gemini peacemaker mode. "My birthday is May twenty-first." He continued without a break. "I'm a zero-degree Gemini with a Virgo moon and Aries rising. I've been told it's an unusual presentation."

"It is, and—"

Stephan shook his head. "Not now." He jerked his chin at Niall. "Best get moving. When will you return, or should we meet elsewhere?"

"I plan to drive back. It will allow me to maximize my telepathy range if I send a repeating message as I travel. I used to live in Denver. Matter of fact, it's the spot I was before I moved to Glenwood Springs a few months back."

"I know many of the local shifters," Stephan said. "Denver is as good a spot to start as any. Angus O'Reilly runs the feedstore, and it has a decent-sized meeting room in the back. I'll let you know if he doesn't agree with using his shop for a gathering spot."

"I'll catch up with you there. Unless I hear otherwise, I'll let everyone know to meet at Angus's as soon as they can." Niall inclined his head in Sarai's direction. "I'd appreciate it if you put a solar return together for me. Haven't had one done for a long time."

"I'd love to." She ignored the way Stephan had narrowed his eyes. "Time and place of birth, please."

"Milford, Ireland, or close enough at ten minutes past three in the morning."

"What year?"

"Aye, that's always a kicker, huh?" Niall transferred his attention to Stephan. "Here's where we discover I should be calling you youngster. I was born in the year of our lord—who's no lord to shifters —1563."

Breath whooshed from her as magic flared around Niall, and he faded into motes of multicolored light. "Did you know how old he was?" she demanded.

Stephan frowned, appearing a little taken aback. "No. He was damned closemouthed about anything on the ship—except charming the next lady in line." He tapped her chest with his index finger. "Mark my words, niece. He'll bring you nothing but heartache. I saw the flare of heat betwixt the two of you. He'll not stand by you past the bedding part."

"What if permanence isn't what I'm looking for?" She tossed her shoulders back. It was long past time for Stephan to stop treating her like an errant daughter in need of direction. Marie's death would only make that tendency worse, and she had to nip it in the bud.

"What are you looking for in a man?" Stephan dropped a hand on her shoulder.

"I don't know, but it's not any of the shifters you and Marie thought were suitable for me." She slithered from beneath his grip. "I'm going into town. I'll meet you at the feedstore in an hour or two."

"We will drive together." Stephan's tone brooked zero possibility of disagreement. "It's not safe. Look what happened to three of us together."

"But we didn't know. We weren't warded." A shudder racked her, followed by another. She didn't want her familiar world to crash down around her head, but she couldn't ignore their narrow escape, either.

"I won't be long." Stephan hurried into the room he'd shared with Marie.

Sarai closed her teeth over her lower lip. Her uncle had just lost the woman he'd loved for well over a century. He had to be grieving, but he wasn't letting pain get in his way. Stephan had an inner strength that cut at least two ways. It made him a formidable ally in any crisis, but it also meant he wasn't particularly flexible in terms of how he viewed the world.

He strode toward her dressed in his usual faded Levi's, a Western shirt, and a woolen jacket. Scuffed cowboy boots graced his feet, and he'd brushed his hair back from his face securing it with a leather thong tied low on his neck.

Sarai placed a hand on his arm. "I don't want to fight with you, and I'm so very sorry about Marie. I loved her too. We'll both miss her terribly."

Stephan offered her a ghost of a smile. "I've never been much of a seer, but I believe these next few months will be hard. Marie may be better off. She hated conflict, and she'd have worried herself silly every time either of us left the house."

"Hiding out is an option, huh?" Sarai dragged a jacket off a hook and slid into it. She slung her bag over one shoulder.

"Yes. We could ward the house and ourselves and let the rest of the world implode around us, but we're not doing that."

He held the door open, and she walked through. They'd never made a habit of locking anything up, but she heard the snick of the deadbolt as her uncle secured their home. It wouldn't slow a vampire down, but then they didn't wander about in broad daylight, either.

He fired the beefy pickup they used to haul everything from hay to stock, and she clambered in on the passenger side. Marie's wildflower scent permeated the cab, and it took effort not to break down sobbing.

"Everything's happening really fast," she murmured.

"It usually does," Stephan agreed, adding, "When magic gets loose, and is used for ill rather than good, events spiral out of control quickly. I was part of the last war with the mages. I was truly young then, not quite twenty, and it opened my eyes to how easily evil gets its claws into a person."

"You never talk about it." Sarai cast a sidelong glance across the cab.

"No reason to cull up unpleasantness. Besides, any talk of the war made Marie uncomfortable. She'd tell me it was long since over and done with, and for me to put it behind me. She assumed magic would never confront its own again, that we'd learned our lesson the first time."

Sarai drew her brows together, thinking. "It's not the only magical war, though. Only the most recent one."

Stephan tightened his grip on the wheel, turning his knuckles white. "This is precisely the reason I insisted on sending you to school once your parents decided you'd be better off with us."

Sarai ground her jaws, remembering. She'd been about fifteen and in full rebellion, shifting in daylight in front of humans. Her father, another wolf shifter and Stephan's brother, got sick and tired of wiping memories. He'd driven her deep into the desert east of Los Angeles one night and dumped her out of the car. She'd been afraid he was going to leave her. Instead, he'd piled out of the car too and shifted, growling a challenge.

She'd thought he wasn't serious until she shifted and understood this was a fight to the death—unless she surrendered.

Surrender wasn't in her vocabulary. Not at her age, so the wolves had tussled and bitten and rolled in the dust until their coats were streaked with blood. Her father's wolf was larger, heavier, but she was more agile. Finally, he got her in a chokehold, jaws poised over her vulnerable neck.

He was so angry, she didn't trust him not to finish her off, so she'd dropped her head to the side, a sign of submission. He'd let her up, but not right away. It was after that, she'd moved in with Stephan and Marie.

"Thank you for taking me in—and for the schooling," she murmured.

"You are quite welcome. My brother is a hothead, but he never gave up on you, never stopped loving you. He still checks up on how you're doing."

"Really?" Her eyes swam with the tears that had been close to the surface since Marie was killed in front of her. "How come I never knew?"

"He didn't want you to, and I honored his wishes."

The truck rattled to a stop. When she looked out the window, she saw the building her shop was in.

"Go on," he urged. "Get out. Be careful to ward yourself. I'll return in about half an hour."

"How'd you know I wanted to come here?"

A smile ghosted around his mouth. "I know you better than you think. You want to consult your arcane bag of tricks—and do a chart for your new friend."

She scooted across the seat and threw her arms around Stephan's neck, kissing his cheek. "Thank you."

"You have your cell phone in that bag?"

"Yeah. The battery is low, but I'll charge it in my shop." She slid toward the passenger door and got out. A quick scan didn't yield any strange magic nearby, but it paid to be careful. Winding a ward around herself, she walked into her building and took the stairs to her basement shop.

Her uncle honked once, and she heard the chug of the truck's diesel engine as he drove away.

She fished in her bag for her keys and unlocked the door to *Sarai's Charms and Crystals*, taking care to secure it behind her. This wasn't a day she wanted to light the open sign.

It was good of Stephan to leave her here. He was a kind man beneath the layer of bluster. She was lucky to have him in her life, and she'd make a point of telling him. Who knew what the next few days would bring?

Moving to a window, she pulled two magical history books from a shelf and began to read. The best way to arm herself for what was coming was to refresh her knowledge of what had gone before. She'd read for a bit, and then she'd feed Niall's information into her computer program. She'd have to insert a few adjustments to accommodate his birth year, but she wanted his chart more than he did.

It would tell her if they were destined for one another.

Her mouth curved into a smile, and her body came alive. She shoved her lascivious thoughts to a distant spot, so she could concentrate on the dry prose spread before her.

CHAPTER 5

Niall nosed the Toyota along I-70's ever-present traffic. His boss at the paramedic company had been so supportive about his mythical grandfather's deteriorating medical condition, he'd felt guilty deceiving her. Lynda Miller had told him to take all the time he needed and not to worry about his job.

Dealing with Lynda reminded him of the last magical war where humans ended up collateral damage. He offered up a quick prayer he'd caught this one in time—at the front end. Today's humans had far more sophisticated weaponry. If they jumped into the game, the outcome would be far worse. Bullets and magic weren't a good mix, particularly when magic redirected those bullets back to the humans who had fired them.

With all the focus on paranormals in television and

the movies, it wouldn't take this batch of humans long to figure out silver-laced bullets, iron swords, and judicious use of salt and holy water solved most of their problems.

He'd done what he could to secure his home with magic, but he'd brought the sabers and hunting knives with him. The wooden jewelry box as well. No reason to leave it for mages or vampires to steal. They could cut through his wards like a hot knife through paraffin. Mostly, his protections were meant to discourage humans.

A neighboring car honked, and he scooted over. He had a long drive ahead, close to three hours if the traffic didn't ease up, and he needed to pay closer attention. Sometimes he missed hansom cabs and horses and wagons. Life then had been simpler, lived at a slower pace, but humankind were all about bigger, better, and faster.

He'd grown used to it, but he didn't like it.

He settled deeper into the car's worn upholstery, avoiding the spring that poked his back, and chuckled. He definitely hadn't fallen for the allure of bigger and better when it came to transportation. He drove old clunkers until something broke that he couldn't fix, and then he bought another one.

As he drove, he thought about Sarai. What a beauty she was. Old enough to have some maturity, but young enough to still be spunky with a decidedly outspoken manner. The hot-tempered ones were hellions in bed. His cock stirred, liking the direction his mind was rolling toward. He rearranged his dick so it wasn't bent double, straining against his snug trousers.

He snorted. He should be mapping battle strategy. Goddess knew he was rusty as hell, but then why shouldn't he be? He hadn't had to think about anything even remotely related to fighting until he tracked the vampires and plotted their destruction. Three vamps were nothing, though, compared with a legion of them fueled by mage power.

It brought up some thorny questions.

Were all the mages involved in this unholy alliance? If not, it would simplify things since shifters could leverage assistance from the ones who hadn't been seduced by vampire trickery.

On the other hand, it was possible mages had approached vampires after plotting a latter-day retaliation for the war, but it seemed unlikely. That conflagration had been over and done with for centuries. Niall curled his brain into a pretzel but couldn't come up with even one good reason for mages to suddenly decide to seek revenge—and the upper hand.

One of the downsides of magic wielders keeping to themselves, though, was he was horribly out of touch with anyone's state of mind beyond his own. These were almost the first vampires he'd seen since migrating to the States. Until today, he'd been convinced they remained in the more southern parts of the country, notably around New Orleans where the voodoo culture was as good a cover as they were likely to find for their bloodsucking ways.

Not that they had a choice. Blood was food for them, but they could remain in a type of stasis for long periods of time. He wasn't sure if they ever exactly died absent severe measures like his iron blades. They'd been a true scourge in earlier centuries. Formed from a pact between the devil and Sekhmet, Egyptian goddess of death and slaughter, they'd proven impossible to eradicate.

And now they'd targeted shifters and figured out a way to steal magic from them. Fury swept through Niall. His stomach tightened, and he forgot his fascination with Sarai—for the moment.

She was impossible to remove from his consciousness for long.

Had this little tableau where vamps shanghaied shifters unfolded elsewhere, or was northern Colorado the pilot site for vampires to test their alliance with mages?

He checked on the telepathic message he had running like a tape loop. No one had replied to him, but part of his message was they didn't need to. Everyone was supposed to head for the feedstore in Denver.

How many would "everyone" comprise? If it was more than a hundred, they'd stick out like a sore thumb. And they wouldn't fit in Angus's establishment. They could always regroup elsewhere. Maybe one of the many ghost towns dotting Colorado's mountains. Quite a few were truly deserted because the roads leading to them had long since fallen to ruin or been wiped out by avalanches.

The more he thought about it, the better he liked the ghost town idea. He shut off the flow of his current telepathy and reached for Stephan. He could use his cell phone, but this was faster and far more private. Besides, he had no idea if Stephan even had a cell phone. Or what the number was.

"Hey, mate. You there?"

"Yes. At Angus's. Where are you?"

"About ninety minutes out, but I had an idea that might keep us flying beneath everyone's locater beacons."

"I'm listening."

Niall rattled off half a dozen ghost towns inaccessible by road.

"It's a good idea. Around fifty of us are already here, and more are arriving every few minutes. Everyone is

pretty spooked, I tell you. Also angry. I'm afraid their combined magic might get out of control."

"Pick a location, and I'll meet you there."

"*Golddust. I have to run by Sarai's shop and grab her, and then we'll head west.*"

Niall sputtered. "*What? You left her alone?*"

"*She's warded. And inside. I'm sure she'll be fine.*"

Niall should leave well enough alone, but he couldn't help himself. "*Get back to me, mate. I have to know she's safe.*"

Stephan was quiet so long, Niall wasn't sure he'd answer. When he did, he said, "*All right. I will. Maybe I misjudged you.*"

"*You didn't. I'm exactly the Lothario you remember, but it doesn't mean I don't have a heart. Or that I can't care.*" Niall cut the connection, not wanting to hear whatever Stephan said next.

He reinstated his earlier telepathic sending with altered instructions and hoped to hell he didn't walk into a group of pissed off shifters who'd started for Denver only to be rerouted.

"Can't be helped," he muttered.

Worry ate at him as most of an hour ticked by with no word from Stephan. A curiosity-tinged interest joined the worry. Why was he so concerned about the wolf shifter? Sure, she was one hot little number, but he'd just met her, and there was no good reason for her to grab a front-and-center focus in his world. He'd never run up against a woman he wanted more than sex and a smidgeon of companionship from. Emphasis on the smidgeon. Once a gal got too clingy, he made it abundantly clear he wasn't that type of fellow.

Was that about to change?

Part of him hoped so, but a far larger part was horrified. He liked his rough-and-tumble way of approaching life, his freedom to snatch a little loving from unlikely candidates. Not that a mate would necessarily curtail his freedom, but if she accorded him permission to fuck where he wished, well then he'd have to do the same.

He gripped the wheel harder. No bloody fucking way would his mate—*his*—screw around on him.

"Aye, there it is. The reason I'm mateless and will continue to be," he murmured to the empty car. "I'm a sodding, unrealistic bloke stuck in centuries-old morals."

He'd nearly reached the turnoff that would take him away from Denver, heading north toward Golddust. As things stood, he was only about thirty minutes from the exit leading to the feedstore.

Despite his stern lecture on why he wasn't good partner material, protectiveness surged. He still couldn't believe Stephan would have left his niece unguarded, especially after what happened to his mate.

If Niall had been there, he wouldn't have let Sarai out of his sight. Perhaps he had ulterior motives, but his primary one would have been to make damn good and certain nothing bad happened to her.

"Stephan!"

The cat shifter didn't answer, so Niall tried again. Still nothing. He signaled and pulled off to the side of the freeway. Easier to employ magic without the car's metal surrounding him. Once he was standing next to the car, he tried again. When Stephan didn't respond, Niall sent magic zinging ahead, but it was wasted effort. He was too far away to sense anything.

He tugged his cell phone from a pocket. Usually he hated the thing, but tonight he was hoping for a miracle. He opened his browser and typed psychic shops+Denver. A list populated, and he scrolled down, anxiously reading each name and wondering if Sarai would have named her store that.

Until he reached *Sarai's Charms and Crystals.*

"Yes!" He fist-pumped the air and noted the address.

He jumped back in the Toyota and gunned it, narrowly missing another car as he careened back into the flow of traffic. He tried to raise Stephan a few more times, but as he drew closer, he quit. If the man had been captured again— Niall blew out a disgusted breath. What kind of fool fell into the same hole twice?

Anyway, if Stephan had been kidnapped again, no point in alerting his captors help was on the way. A mage was more than capable of forcing a telepathic link with Stephan, and Niall hoped his earlier broadcast about the location of the shifters' meeting place hadn't been intercepted.

He silently blessed his wisdom in bringing the iron blades. He'd nearly left them behind, mostly because they'd be hard to explain if one of Colorado's finest pulled him over for speeding, something he was frequently guilty of.

He dragged the phone out again and tapped the navigation program, using the voice feature to feed in Sarai's address. A tinny female British bot told him where to turn and how to avoid traffic jams. Even with her assistance, it took him almost twenty minutes before he pulled up a discrete two blocks from Sarai's shop.

Exiting the car, he probed with magic, keeping a delicate hand. No reason to blast enough power to alert any magic wielder within a half-mile radius of his presence. Elation surged when he was almost certain he got a hit off Sarai's unique energy—and her uncle's. Threading more power, he checked again, wanting to be sure.

This wasn't like charging vampires in the middle of nowhere. He needed a wee bit more subtlety and stealth in a crowded neighborhood. Niall walked behind the Toyota and opened the trunk, intent on grabbing the same blade he'd used earlier. He'd appreciated its heft and its follow-through as he swung it.

Lights flared from behind him. He waited for the car to drive past, except it was moving really slowly. And then it stopped. A spotlight flared and a robust, "You all right there, fellow?" augmented by an electronic speaker was so loud it hurt his ears. The light would have been worse if it was after dark.

He slammed the trunk. "Aye, mate. Quite well. I'd be even better if you'd stop trying to blind and deafen me."

A uniformed man got out of the squad car. "Sorry. Standard procedure. Looking for something in your trunk?"

"As it happens I was. A tire gauge. Right front's looking a wee bit on the flat side." Niall threaded suggestion beneath his words. Everything was fine here. All the cop needed to do was move on.

The tall, thin officer dressed in a beige uniform and carting a full gun belt walked closer, eying Niall. "Humph. Figured you might be drunk and hunting for another bottle."

"Sure and my family are a right bunch of boozers, but the bug never bit me." Niall laid on the brogue and stepped aside. "Feel free to have a looksee inside. You won't be finding aught of interest." He pulled the passenger door open and upped the ante on his subliminal suggestions.

"Thanks." The cop bent and looked inside, shining a flashlight over the beat-up interior of Niall's car. "I'll be damned. You didn't lie to me."

"Why would I?" Niall smiled as he chivied the officer with still more magic, desperate to have him get back in his car and leave.

The man must have felt his last blast of compulsion because he shook his head, staggering a little as he retraced his steps, got into his cruiser, and took off without so much as a backward glance.

Niall didn't waste time feeling guilty. Worst the cop would have tomorrow was a headache, while the ten minutes he'd just wasted might mean Sarai and her uncle had been spirited away.

Or killed.

He ran back to the trunk, snatched up the saber, and locked his car before moving as fast as he dared toward Sarai's shop. He shrouded himself, blending into the afternoon as best he could. No one should see him, unless they looked with magic of their own.

He'd memorized her address, and when the building came into view, he rocked back on the balls of his feet taking stock. Her shop was in one of those multistory affairs housing many different businesses. He could figure out which one was hers on the directory inside, but this type of structure offered far too many places to hide.

Although, that could work in his favor as well.

He risked another scan, breathing a sigh of relief that she was still inside. He waited until two people—a couple with their arms around one another—cleared the main entrance before walking through it. A few folks milled around the foyer, but not one of them glanced his way, which told him his enchantment was working.

Someone as tall as he was carting a medieval weapon would be sure to draw at least a few surprised stares—even in the middle of a city as sophisticated as Denver.

He stopped in front of the directory both to locate Sarai's shop and to memorize the layout of the building. She was on the lowest level, which at least meant a ready exit without risking jumping from three floors up. Easy for his jaguar, more challenging in his current form. Too bad the cat couldn't swing the iron blade.

A chuckle from within told him his bondmate was ready and waiting. It loved a good fight even more than he did.

Intent on maintaining the element of surprise as

long as possible, he slid into a stairwell and ran down one flight, taking the steps three and four at a time. As he'd expected, the corridor was deserted since most humans were lazy and preferred elevators.

He sidled into the downstairs hall, looking left and right. The stench of vampire hit him almost immediately. He gave Stephan an F for judgment, except he was here too, and clearly paying for the folly of leaving his niece unguarded. Niall dug deeper and caught a whiff of mage magic. No mages here, but the vamps must have borrowed liberally from them to allow them to strike in full daylight.

Damn. That was unfortunate news. If he couldn't count on vampires limiting their offensives to the dark of night, it compounded his problems a hundredfold.

Sarai's shop was at the very end of an empty hallway. Even though most humans couldn't sense magic, something about the ambiance down here would send most all of them scuttling for a place that didn't make the small hairs on the backs of their necks quiver.

"*Hurry,*" his jaguar urged.

Niall trusted his cat's instincts. He dropped his invisibility illusion and focused all his power on the upcoming confrontation. A growl followed by a snarl sent him running to Sarai's door. He angled a blast of magic to unlatch it and charged through.

Sarai was in wolf form, moving so fast her body was a gray and black blur. Two vamps were quick, but she was faster. A high-pitched bark drove the vamps back from where Stephan sprawled on the floor in a spreading pool of blood. He wasn't dead, not yet, anyway.

Magic flowed, thick and viscous. A perimeter shot with lightning bolts formed around Stephan, creating mini-explosions when shifter magic collided with vampire power.

Time to end this charade. Niall swung the blade, slashing through the nearest vamp's neck. Black ichor spewed, stinking of a charnel pit, but he was getting used to how they died. He took aim at the second vamp, but it took on an insubstantial aspect.

"Bloody hell, you are *not* leaving," he shouted and focused magic to hold the creature from Hell in place long enough to end it forever.

He hefted the blade and brought it down squarely atop the vampire's head. The vertical gash went from crown to sternum as he split the abomination wide open.

Power flared blue-white out of the corner of one eye; Sarai was human again and kneeling over Stephan's inert form. Magic poured from her outstretched hands as she probed for damage with healing enchantments.

Niall kicked the door shut. No reason to give some poor unfortunate sod nightmares for the rest of his natural life. He didn't expect humans, not with all the power floating about, but someone might be drunk or stoned enough to blunder through all the warning signs.

He joined Sarai on the floor. She'd turned Stephan over and added a few crystals to her healing efforts. They glowed in a bevy of shades. The vamps were already turning to smoking piles of bone and dust. Too bad their hideous black blood never vanished along with their flesh.

"What happened?" he asked Sarai.

"What didn't?" she countered. "Help me with my uncle. I'm almost done."

"Tell me what to do. Healing isn't exactly my forte."

"Open your magic to me."

He forged a channel between them, holding it open and acutely aware of her nakedness. Her body was as close to perfection as anything he'd ever seen, and her musky vanilla scent cut through the vampire stench. He ached to run his fingertips over her silky skin, so he clasped his hands in his lap to counteract the temptation. With all the power oozing from her, she'd taken on an iridescent glow that made her looks otherworldly. Like a goddess.

Sarai straightened. "There. He'll come around soon. Thank god the bites were superficial."

"What happened?" Niall repeated, needing to know. "We have to get out of here before more of them show up."

She pushed to her feet and picked her way around dead vampire and pools of ichor to a cabinet against the back wall. Opening it, she pulled out clothing and proceeded to dress. "I was doing research when I sensed vamps closing in. Since things went so badly with me in my human body, I shifted. What's left of my clothes are somewhere beneath that mess." She pointed at the vampire remains.

"Weren't you warded?" Niall tried for an even tone. He didn't want to come across as critical.

"Yes, but I didn't trust it. Not totally, and I'm stronger as a wolf." She blew out a tight breath and slid her feet into running shoes, leaving the laces untied. "I'd no sooner shifted than they blasted through my door as if it wasn't locked. They lunged for me, but between my ward and my wolf, they couldn't grab me."

She inhaled raggedly. "Their fangs were out. Ready. Christ but I was scared. I should have left the back window open. If I had, I could have jumped out of it and been gone. I was plotting a way out, edging around them to position myself close to the door, but then Uncle showed up. The minute they saw him, they ignored me. One of them latched onto his neck.

"He yelled at me to take my chance and run, but no way in hell would I have left him here by himself."

Niall inclined his head in respect. "You are one gutsy woman."

"No, I'm not. I was so scared my legs were shaking even as a wolf. I jumped on the vamp that had Stephan. Bit him as hard as I could." She made a face. "They taste worse than they smell. I spit out all the blood I could. I know it's bad to drink from them, but who would want to? It shook me off, so I leapt on the other one. Anything so they'd leave Stephan alone.

"I was switching from one to the other, trying to keep them too busy to drink from Uncle again, when you showed up." She latched her gaze onto his. "It's the second time you've saved my life today. And Stephan's. Thank you."

Niall picked his way across her shop until he stood next to her. He balanced the blade against a bookshelf and opened his arms but didn't say anything.

She looked him up and down, from head to feet, taking his measure before she walked into his embrace and folded her arms around him. He held her trembling body against him murmuring in Gaelic as an imperative to shield her now and always raced through him.

With protectiveness came possessiveness—and knowledge. This woman was different. She was someone he wanted by his side, not just in his bed, although he longed for her that way as well.

He buried his hands in her hair, turned her face upward, and covered her mouth with his. After a heart wrenchingly long moment, she kissed him back, all heat and fire with nibbles, bites, and her tongue jammed into his mouth as she molded the length of her body to his. Her nipples formed stiff peaks against his chest, and his cock surged to attention wanting more than the warmth of her belly.

Stephan groaned from his spot on the floor.

Niall broke their kiss and offered a rakish grin. "We need to get out of here, but hold onto those impulses. If the goddess grants us grace, we'll find a spot of solitude to love one another."

Her lips, beautiful lips soft from their kisses, parted in a vixen's smile. "I'd like that."

He started to launch into telling her how lovely she was, but this wasn't the time. Danger was far too close.

Stephan was on his feet. "Come on," he urged. "Ditch the romantic crap. Let's teleport to Golddust."

Niall grabbed the saber with one hand and Sarai with the other. "We'll drive partway," he said. "My car's close."

Stephan didn't disagree. "Probably just as well. My

magic is sucking fumes." He turned to Sarai. "Why didn't you leave when I told you?"

"Maybe because I didn't want to live with your death on my conscience. I'm not a coward, Uncle."

His blue-eyed gaze softened. "I love you. I wanted you to be safe."

She wrapped her arms around him. "I know. But that street runs both ways."

Niall cracked the door. The hall was still deserted. He motioned Sarai and Stephan through, and all of them ran for the door marked *Exit*. No reason to return to the lobby. None at all.

They made it to his Toyota, and he fired the engine, intent on driving as far as they could before the dirt road to Golddust became impassable. Teleport spells were power pigs, and he had a feeling they'd need to marshal their resources for an inevitable showdown.

Just his luck. He'd finally found a woman who lit his soul on fire when shifters faced their worst problem in several hundred years. He might not live through it. She might not, either.

Maybe he should hold off on his declaration of caring, of maybe even wanting her for his mate, until this was over. It might make him a coward, but he'd never viewed himself as mate material. He had a lot of explaining to do, justifications for his man-whore ways, and the task felt daunting.

"*That's right*," the jaguar blurted from the sidelines.

"*What's right?*"

"*Go hide behind a rock like you always do.*"

"*What's that supposed to mean?*"

"What does your jaguar want?" Sarai asked from where she sat next to him.

"Nothing. It's always chatty after we've faced danger."

She sent a penetrating look his way but didn't say anything more.

He tried out and discarded words to add to what he'd said, but every combination would just dig him in deeper. For all his womanizing faults, he was honest, and he wouldn't compound the half lie he'd already told Sarai by piling another on top of it.

CHAPTER 6

Sarai was thrilled when Niall stood close, arms extended. She wanted the comfort of his arms, wanted her body plastered the length of his. Yet, she took a moment to gather her thoughts. She'd felt the desire spilling through him when she'd drawn magic to work on Stephan, but he hadn't taken advantage of their proximity.

Even now, he was offering her a choice. He hadn't simply pulled her into an embrace. She breathed in his scent, a clean forest-after-rain smell that soothed and inflamed her by turns. Only a step separated them, but when she took it she felt she'd crossed a huge divide.

One where there'd be no going back.

She twined her arms around him, splaying her hands over the slabs of muscle running down his back. When he closed his arms around her and drew her as close as they could be, a shock of hunger arrowed right into her soul. The sensation was so raw and primitive, it stunned her.

When he cradled her head in his big hands, she didn't fight him, welcoming his mouth as he kissed her. It had been so long since she'd been kissed, it took her a moment to kiss him back. The feel of his mouth, hard and demanding, called to her, the summons urgent and laced with untrammeled need.

She opened her mouth to him, aware her nipples had turned to hot points of sensation. His cock hardened against her belly, and an image of it flashed through her mind from when he'd been naked in the clearing with his manhood proudly displayed.

If her uncle wouldn't have been a few feet away, she'd probably have pushed her pants down her legs and bent over the nearby writing table. She wanted him, needed him, and her heart thudded into double-time rhythm.

She was about to reach between them, desperate to wrap her fingers around his girth, when her uncle groaned.

Niall lifted his mouth from hers and grinned. "We need to get out of here but hold onto those impulses. If the goddess grants us grace, we'll find a spot of solitude to love one another."

She smiled back, not wanting to let go of him. "I'd like that."

Stephan scrambled to his feet. "Come on," he urged. "Ditch the romantic crap. Let's teleport to Golddust."

"Are you sure you're all right?" Sarai asked.

"Good enough to leave here."

Niall disentangled from their embrace and took her hand. "We'll drive partway. My car's close."

She waited for Stephan to lodge a protest, but he didn't disagree. "Probably just as well," he muttered. "My magic is sucking fumes." He turned to her. "Why didn't you leave when I told you?"

"Maybe because I didn't want to live with your death on my conscience. I'm not a coward, Uncle."

Stephan's normally stern expression softened. "I love you. I wanted you to be safe."

She picked her way through gore and bone bits not wanting to even think how much work cleaning her shop would be. When she got to Stephan, she let go of Niall's hand and wrapped her arms around her uncle. "I know. But that love stuff cuts both ways."

Niall cracked the door, probably checking the hall, but she didn't sense any other vampires or mages anywhere in the vicinity. Seemingly satisfied, he herded them through. They ran for the exit door on her floor.

Once outside, he set a decent pace, quick but not so fast as to draw undue attention. He placed himself between her and Stephan, partially shielding the saber from view.

Weariness dragged at her as she settled into the saggy passenger seat. Her uncle got into the back and stretched out as much as his six-foot-three-inch frame would allow.

After they were underway, Niall eyed Stephan through the rearview mirror. "I've had a nap or two back there. It's not so bad once you find a spot where the springs don't poke you."

"Not there yet," Stephan grunted.

Sarai faded in and out as they drove. Bumps in the road and traffic noise woke her, but not for long. At one point, she felt magic flare as Niall and his jaguar talked, but when she asked what the sleek, tawny cat wanted, Niall had hedged. She hadn't had magic deployed, but she was certain he'd waltzed around the point.

It's none of my business.

Yeah but, he could have...

Could have what? Told her to butt out? Told her a kiss didn't mean sharing everything?

She shuttered her thoughts, not wanting him to poke into her mind. She might have suggested to Stephan that she could enjoy Niall's body without expecting more, but she'd never been that type. Not that she hadn't savored her occasional roll in the hay, but she'd picked her partners carefully, avoiding men who had potential as more than a momentary diversion.

Crap on a piece of toast, I'm as broken as he is.

Eh, maybe not. He's upfront about his proclivities, while I conceal my liaisons.

Niall had turned off the freeway a while back. After a particularly robust bump, he pulled to the side of a badly rutted road, killed the engine, and said, "We'll teleport from here."

"Good idea." Stephan pushed one of the Toyota's back doors open amid the creak of rusty hinges.

"Where is Golddust?" she asked as she prodded her own door open and got out. "I've never been there." Other cars lined the road, which meant shifters were converging in the abandoned mining town. At least, she hoped that was what it meant. Light leached from the day, and it would be fully dark soon.

Full dark meant vampires would be running at maximum velocity.

"About ten more miles down this road," Niall replied, joining her. He'd been quiet since his offhanded comment about his bondmate being chatty after they faced danger.

A ratty, falling-down town flashed across her mind. "Got it," she said and summoned magic.

"Hold on, sister." Stephan hooked a hand beneath her arm.

"I'll be fine." She bristled and almost added she probably could have given the vamps the slip if he hadn't shown up, but she didn't want to hurt his feelings. Something nagged. When she figured out what it was, she shook free from her uncle's grip.

"Goddammit! I should have noticed this before, but how could those vampires attack in daylight?"

"They were running on mage power." Stephan spat the answer. "Didn't you sense the other magic?"

"I did." Niall nodded curtly. "It didn't matter. They were going down no matter whose magic they filched."

Sarai's jaw gaped open. "B-but it means we're not safe in the daytime, either."

"That's exactly what it means," Niall said, his voice grim as a doomsday prophecy. "These vamps were stronger than the ones cowering in the back of that cabin, so they're becoming more proficient at leveraging mage power."

"All good reasons we shouldn't hang around here." Stephan grabbed her arm again. "Group teleport spell, people."

This time, she didn't fight free from his fingers curving around her upper arm. The ramifications of fighting vampires 24/7 had sunk in, and she wanted to curl up in a ball of misery and howl her desolation to the skies.

"*Buck up*," her wolf ordered. "*No surrender. Not with me as your bonded one.*"

"This time, it's your bond animal who's talking," Niall observed and took hold of her other arm.

"Right you are," she retorted, not offering any clues as to its lecture. Giving up was easier than fighting until something killed her, but she hadn't seriously considered it. Not really. Mostly, she was tired. And numb. And confused about her feelings for Niall.

She didn't know him all that well. Why should what he did matter one way or the other? The men's spell rose around her. When it cleared, they were in the midst of a whole lot of shifters. More than she'd ever seen in one place before. Everyone was talking at once.

Niall and Stephan threaded their way through the crowd, tapping a shoulder here, shaking a hand there. She followed them, not wanting to be left behind. Because trust was running thin, she scattered power, assessing the assembled crowd. At least vampires weren't lurking in the wings, but she did sense something other than shifter magic coming from the end of what had once been the main street through Golddust.

She caught up to Niall and Stephan and said,

"Check dead ahead and to the right." She purposefully didn't employ telepathy in case someone was listening to the conversations unfolding all around her.

Both men stopped dead. Power arced from them. Niall swore, "Son of a bitch," and took off running calling shifters by name to follow him.

By the time she got to where she'd sensed the intrusive magic and worked her way around the crowd that had formed in front of a dilapidated hotel, Niall, Stephan, and others she didn't know had dragged half a dozen men and women into the street. Now that the interlopers weren't warded, mage power steamed from them.

"Talk and talk fast," Niall hissed.

Shifters circled the six mages, hemming them in and draping magic around them so they couldn't leave. Echoes of, "Talk," rippled from many mouths.

One of the male mages squared his shoulders. Tall and rangy, he was dressed in jeans, boots, and a leather jacket. Blond hair was cropped close to his skull, and he tilted his chin at a defiant angle. Blue eyes flashed a challenge. "We're on your side."

"But we didn't expect you to believe us, so we hid." A blonde woman who might have been the man's twin planted herself next to him.

"Go ahead. Set a truth spell around us," the man urged. "I'm Jeremiah. My sister is Chloe. We're just as horrified by the vampires' doings as you are. And by our kin becoming their allies."

"The magic surrounding you already contains a truth casting," Stephan noted in a somber tone.

"Aye. You did speak the truth. At least as far as it went," Niall muttered.

Sarai pushed forward. "Do you know how many mages allied themselves with vampires?"

"Maybe," Jeremiah replied. "A small group are still angry about the outcome of the last war. They call themselves Mages First and hold regular meetings."

"Since when?" Stephan asked.

Chloe shrugged. Her hair hung in braids reaching knee level, and she wore dark pants and a tattered green ski parka. "Forever. From what I gathered, the group formed soon after our ship reached the Americas."

Interesting. So they arrived on separate vessels.

"Is this Mages First group nationwide?" Niall asked.

"Yes and no," Jeremiah answered. "It was much bigger two hundred years ago, but people's interest waned. "From what we can tell, the largest concentration is in northern Texas these days."

"Define large," Stephan growled.

"I'd be surprised if a hundred were left," Chloe replied.

"It may not sound like a very big number," Jeremiah cut in, "but locating them and severing them from their magic will be a huge undertaking."

Chloe exhaled sharply. "Indeed. We performed that rite on three of our own, and it took a week for our magic to recover."

Sarai was fascinated—and repelled. She'd had no idea there was a way to separate a magic wielder from the source of their power, absent killing them. Which brought up a point. "Why not just kill them and be done with it?"

Chloe turned sad blue eyes her way. "They're our kinsmen."

Sarai understood. Mowing down her family in cold blood would take more fortitude than she possessed. Killing vampires was one thing. She had no idea if she had it in her to plunge a knife into a shifter's chest, especially knowing its bond animal would be trapped in limbo for eternity.

Niall motioned the six mages forward. "How did you find out about our meeting? Who else knows you're here?"

A short redheaded male said, "We've been monitoring magical frequencies ever since the incident in Glenwood Springs the other night where innocent humans lost their lives."

"Was that the first time vamps stole mage magic and used it for ill?" Someone behind Sarai shouted.

"Insofar as we know," the man responded.

"There's a piece of decent news," Niall muttered, adding, "That explains how you knew about our meeting. Who knows you're here?"

"All our mage kin who walk the good side of the street," Chloe answered.

"We knew showing up in your midst would be dangerous," Jeremiah cut in, "so we used a lottery to select who would come."

"We figured you'd discover us," the redhead said.

Something bothered Sarai. "Since you're apparently innocent, why were you hiding?"

Color stained Jeremiah's stubbled cheeks. "We're not warriors. We were scared what you'd do to us. You have every right to be angry."

"We were planning to show ourselves," Chloe said. "As soon as all of you had arrived and it appeared you had a plan in place."

"We willingly offer our magic to the cause." The redhead stood as tall as his stature allowed. Dressed in jeans, boots, and a leather jacket like many of them, his tone was serious.

"How about the others who aren't here?" Niall asked. "Will they stand with us?"

"Most of them," Jeremiah said.

"We never were very hardy fighters," Chloe added with a wry head shake. "Could be why we lost the war in the Old Country. Very few mages have a taste for battle. We'd rather lose ourselves in spells and books."

Sarai had been listening carefully and testing their words with her own magic in addition to the truth spell fluttering around them. Because the mages knew about it, there'd been no reason to make it invisible. So far, everything the mages had said pinged cleanly off her radar. Maybe this vampire uprising wouldn't be as impossible to quell as she'd feared. Mages might not want to kill their own, but shifters wouldn't be bound by such compunctions.

She gathered saliva, still tasting vampire on her tongue, and spat it out. The taste was fading, but it tied her guts into knots.

"We still need a plan." Niall projected his voice with magic.

"Yes, and a way to reach every single shifter and warn them to be vigilant," Stephan tossed out.

"Our people are in danger as well," Chloe noted.

Sarai frowned. "Can they be co-opted against their will?"

Jeremiah nodded. "It begins against their will, but we've never been especially strong when it came to vampire coercion, which is why we settled where they weren't."

"What happened?" Sarai asked.

Chloe shrugged. "They came looking for us. We're not hard to find, and they apparently knew about Mages First because that's who they started with."

"Aye, and it's who we'll finish with," Niall growled.

An idea took form based on something Sarai had read in the shifter history tome, and she said, "Not much point in kidnapping a mage, even a Mages First one, but what if we capture a vampire?"

Niall quirked a brow. "What would we do with it?"

"Torture it. Hope it calls its dark brothers for rescue."

Stephan clapped her on the back. "Nice, bloodthirsty plan, niece. When they show up, we kill them."

Sarai nodded. "If they're all connected, it should make the others so angry, they come gunning for us."

"And then we do away with them too. I like it. A two-step plan where we knock out enough vamps to discourage them and every single Mages First member we can lay our hands on." Niall narrowed his eyes and focused his next words on the crowd. "How many of you hung onto the old sabers?"

A scattering of hands went up.

"We can teleport and return with weaponry," a silver-haired shifter said.

"Do it," Niall replied. "Return as soon as you can. Maybe by then we'll have located a vampire."

"Or lured one," Sarai said. "The other advantage of my plan is we get to pick where events unfold. We could remain where we are. It's far enough from civilization, there wouldn't be any human casualties."

"May we put out the call for our mage brethren?" Jeremiah asked.

Stephan nodded. "Make very sure of whom you're including."

"No worries there. It's our hides on the line too. Last thing we want is to resurrect the war between us." Power bubbled around the mages as they employed telepathy.

Sarai moved off to one side, intent on fleshing out the easiest way to snag a vampire. When it came to her, she felt like an idiot because it was obvious. Only problem was the men wouldn't like it much, and she needed them to pull it off.

Maybe she'd start with Niall, since she figured Stephan would blow a gasket. She waited until Niall was done talking with an eagle shifter and then crooked a finger his way. When he strode to her side, she said, "I've got it."

"Got what, darling?"

Her eyes widened with pleasure at the endearment, but she didn't comment on it. "Simplest way to find a vampire is to return to either the cabin or my shop. If you're right about them all being linked to one another, they'll sense we've returned to where we killed their own, and they'll be all over it."

"Grand idea, except you're not going."

"The hell I'm not. It's my plan."

He dropped his hands onto her shoulders and spun her to face him. "It's a decent approach, and it's also damned dangerous. I'll take a few of the men so we'll have enough firepower to subdue whoever shows up. It won't only be one vampire. They always travel in packs, which means we need to kill all but one and keep him from teleporting out of there. It will be a delicate balancing act requiring split-second timing—"

She tried to duck from beneath his hands, but he held her in place. "Damn it. Let go of me. If I was a man you'd take me."

"Maybe. Depends how strong your magic was. Now, be a good lass and get some sleep. You're dead on your feet and have every right to be."

Sarai tamped down fury. Her wolf howled within, mirroring her mood. "Fine." She tossed her head. "I'll duck into one of those buildings, and—"

His fingers bit deeper, and he transferred one hand to her upper arm and began marching between two buildings. "You're as transparent as the day is long."

"Where are you taking me?" She kept pace with

him because she didn't want anyone to think he was dragging her against her will.

He didn't answer, just kept on walking until they stood next to a secluded glade behind what had once been the local saloon. He turned her back to face him. Emotions rippled across his stunning features, but she couldn't interpret any of them.

"We have a wee bit of breathing space before everyone returns with swords and sabers and whatever they kept from olden times." He kept talking. "I know the look in those blue eyes of yours. You were planning to teleport out of here and do your own reconnaissance."

She looked away from his direct gaze. It had been exactly what she'd planned. Further, she hadn't given up. She needed to find a way to make him trust she'd be compliant, and then she'd be gone.

"At least denials aren't spewing from you." He maintained a firm grip on her upper arms. Heat from his hands seared her, made her yearn for his body molded to hers.

Twin flames kindled in the depths of his eyes, and they developed the silvery patina from when he'd charged into the remote cabin. His scent intensified, and she didn't need to look down for evidence of his desire. It rose around them, hot and compelling, impossible to deny.

She ached for him too. Defiance bled out of her, replaced by a far more primitive need. Why did she chase away people who cared about her? What was wrong with her?

"It's the same problem I have," he murmured, having clearly been inside her mind. "We're afraid to open ourselves. Afraid to be vulnerable." He swallowed, his throat working. "I don't know what it is about you, but I want you like I've never wanted another woman. And not just for the pleasure we can bring one another."

"My uncle said you had a silver tongue." It was hard to talk since every drop of moisture in her body had headed south, slicking her female bits with desire.

"Aye, that I do, but in this case, I mean every word."

Slow, deliberate, he lowered his head and slashed his mouth over hers.

CHAPTER 7

Niall hadn't planned to tell her how much she meant to him, but her combination of savageness and vulnerability called to kindred places within him. He couldn't not have kissed her even if he'd tried to hold back. Driven by need, want, lust, and a lifetime of repressing every single emotion that might have ended up with him mated, fierceness erupted in their kiss.

Their bodies crashed together, and they grappled with one another. The tang of lust grew bolder as a Bacchanalian tableau raced through his mind, each scene more graphic than the next.

He wrapped his arms around Sarai, exploring her back with hands desperate to discover every inch of her. Moving lower, he ended up cupping the amazing roundness of her high, firm ass. A man could die for an ass like that, and he imagined taking her from behind. She was tall enough, they could do it standing with him driving into her, a breast in either hand as they fucked.

Excitement built, and he pulled her tight against his erection, butting it into her belly as he fantasized the slick tightness of her vault around him.

Their kiss deepened, intensified as their tongues sparred and kisses escalated to bites and nips. Deep within him, his jaguar purred in a low, erotic rumble right before it shrieked a mating challenge, shocking him.

Niall should let go of Sarai. He should run.

The mating cry was both prophecy and promise. If he made love with the woman in his arms, it would seal their bond as surely as if they'd stood before a shaman in the ancient shifter mating ritual.

Her eyes flashed open, and she tore her mouth from his, breathing hard. "You heard that, right?"

"Aye." He let go of her to-die-for ass and cupped one side of her face in a hand. "Do you fully understand its meaning?"

She reared back but couldn't get far because one of his arms still circled her. "Of course I do. It's the mate bond." She shook herself. "It's permanent, right?"

Niall nodded. Had he lost his mind? Of all the

times to take on a mate, this wasn't one of them. Not with everything they faced.

She looked away, but it didn't change the desire spilling from her, turning the air incandescent with sexual heat. "Can't we, uh, do this without triggering the bond?"

"Nay, darling. It's gone too far. If we make love, we'll be mates." He took a deep breath before reciting words that would bind them, ancient words spoken by every pair of shifter bondmates. "I want you to become my mate, Sarai, through this life and all others. Will you have me?"

She tilted her head, locking her gaze onto his. "I, uh, I'm not sure. It's too soon. We don't know each other very well. We—"

Rather than telling her she was lost in twenty-first century sensibilities, that the mate bond took care of everything essential and it could strike within minutes of a shifter couple meeting, he bent his head and kissed her again. Slow. Lazy. Full of the potential of everything they could be to one another.

Reticent at first, she yielded to his kiss, opening her mouth and pressing her body against his. Still locked in an embrace, he walked them deeper into the shadows and slid a hand beneath her jacket and top. His fingers connected with the silky heat of her back.

"Will you have me?" he repeated.

"Yes." Her response was choked, breathless, but it kicked the door wide open.

He didn't think he could be much more aroused, but the touch of her body ignited him, and what little self-control was left frittered to nothing. He repositioned his hand, brushing it over her ribcage until he'd filled it with a breast. The erect nipple begged to be touched; he rolled it between a thumb and forefinger until a low, desperate moan emerged from her. She reached between them and curled her fingers around the throbbing hardness trapped by his too-tight pants.

Torn by duty to the shifters waiting to strike and desire for the woman in his arms, Niall ripped his mouth from hers. He hadn't meant for them to make love, but he hadn't anticipated the mating urge taking over, either.

His breath came fast in little panting blasts. "I would like our first time to be in more elegant surroundings, not grappling in the dirt. We can stop now, but we're far from done with one another. If we live through the war that's nearly upon us, we can pick up where we left off."

Sarai shook her head. Her blue eyes had darkened to midnight with silvery flecks around the pupils, courtesy of her dual nature. "But we might not survive. I'm scared of commitment. You were right about that, but I'm ready to face that fear and leave it behind me. It's why I told you yes."

She hadn't let go of his cock, and she added her other hand to work his button and zipper open. "We can't be gone long. The shifters need you, and I promise not to go off on my own like a madwoman."

His pants were open, and she drew his more-than-hard appendage out. The feel of her hands on his sensitive flesh almost blew the top of his head off. When she fell to her knees in front of him and took him into her mouth, he stopped thinking. Gripping her head in both hands he drove into her, having moved beyond everything but the sensation thundering through him.

She ran her fingertips the length of his shaft, teasing, squeezing, working him. All the while, her tongue swirled around the tip at the top of every stroke. He was lost, drowning, and he wouldn't last long. Not with the wicked dance her tongue was doing.

The only thing missing was touching her. He had to touch her, feel the magic of her body beneath his fingers. He drew himself out of her mouth and tumbled them onto the ground. It was cold and rocky, so he lay on his back to shield her from the worst of it and pulled her thick sweatpants down her legs. Her unlaced shoe popped off, but it gave her one leg free, enough to sit astride him.

She threw a leg over him, straddling his hips. The sight of her above him, half-dressed like a hoyden stoked his excitement. He curved his hands around her slender waist and lowered her onto his erection. Her vault snugged around him, all fire and slickness and scorching wonder.

Sarai tugged his shirt and jacket up and spread her body atop his, skin to skin with her sinfully delicious breasts squashed between them. He wanted to savor her, take this slow, but slow wasn't in the cards. Not with his cat yowling and her wolf howling. He linked to her magic to complete their coupling and thrust into her hard, deep, fast, sure.

She fucked him back. Somewhere along the path, their mouths ended up glued together breath mingling as they panted and ground and strained against one another. Because he was joined with her magically, he sensed her arousal, knew when something he did pushed her higher.

And he wanted her as high as she could go.

He tried to hold her just on the brink, but they were both too excited, and she dissolved around him in a rush of contractions that triggered his own release. Orgasm had never felt so intense as semen juddered from him.

They rocked against one another for long moments as their passion receded. Niall crooned to her, told her he'd love her forever. Protect her forever. He rolled them onto their sides, not wanting to leave the tender promise of her body.

"We should get back," she murmured, "although I don't want to go."

Her words, evidence she cared for him, needed him, wanted him were a balm. He held her tight and kissed her forehead before beginning to disentangle himself.

Footsteps pounded toward them. He sensed Stephan's energy and winced. Would Sarai's uncle challenge him to open warfare? If Niall had followed protocol, he'd have secured Stephan's permission before mating with his niece. Sex pure and simple required no such ceremony.

"Damn it." Sarai rolled away from him and tugged her pants up her legs before retrieving the errant shoe. "He'll know."

Niall set his own clothing to rights and zipped himself back into his pants, not an easy task since he was still mostly hard. "Sure and he will. Mated sex has its own scent. Sarai, look at me."

She turned his way as she put on her shoe, lacing both of them this time.

"I meant everything I said. We belong to each other now, and I wouldn't change a thing about any of it."

A smile began in her eyes and spread to her mouth.

"Neither would I. See, that's the thing about being scared of something. Until you face it, you don't understand why you were scared in the first place."

"Being mated is a big step," he teased.

"Or a small one. I feel like I've been waiting for you my whole life."

Niall's heart split wide open, and his cat yowled its joy.

Stephan raced toward them, stopping precipitously a few feet away. "There you are," he began, followed by, "Goddess be damned. You didn't."

Sarai rose to her feet. Her red hair was a wild nest, and her face still bore bite and kiss marks, plus it had turned a lovely rose shade from her orgasm. She bowed her head. "We did. We are mated, Uncle. I should have secured your permission, but—"

Stephan tilted his head, scenting the air. A broad smile spread across his face. "So you are. Well then, my worries about Niall were groundless." He stretched out a hand. Niall scrambled upright and shook it. "Welcome to the family, son. No way out."

"I'm not looking for one." Niall released Stephan's hand. "You were hunting me for a reason. What's happened in the half hour Sarai and I stole for ourselves?"

He should apologize for not offering the vampire problem his full concentration, but he'd be damned if he'd say he was sorry. What had happened between him and Sarai felt right, necessary. He meant what he'd told her, that he wouldn't change what just flowed between them, wouldn't trade it for all the world's riches.

"Micah's in trouble," Stephan said without preamble.

"Who's he?" Sarai asked.

"The coyote shifter with silver hair. He went to retrieve a saber."

"Aye, I remember him," Niall said. "What kind of trouble?"

"Vampires are in his house. They drained his wife and two children. He wasn't able to tell Jeremiah more before the telepathy cut off."

Niall squared his shoulders. "We have to go to him."

"My take too," Stephan said. "I have five men including me, but we need you and your weapons."

"Are any of the mages coming?" Sarai asked, followed by, "Why didn't Micah's wife accompany him to Golddust?"

"Affirmative on the mages. Jeremiah will be joining us. Micah's wife wasn't a shifter." Stephan's words were laced with disapproval. Marriage to humans was common enough, but far from an accepted practice.

"We need to hurry." Niall started toward Stephan.

"I'm coming." Sarai loped after him.

"Not wise, niece—" Stephan began.

"Aye, darling. I'll fight better if I know you're safe," Niall stopped shy of adding compulsion to his words. He'd be cursed five times over before he'd exert that kind of control over his brand-new mate.

She tossed her head back and drew herself up tall. "Nowhere is safe. Not here. Not anywhere. We're mated. I need to be by your side." She grinned crookedly. "Read your own history books. They're clear enough in that regard. Mates fight next to one another."

"Since when do scrolls take the place of common sense?" Stephan muttered and trained his can't-squirm-out-from-under-this-look Niall's way. "She's your mate. Decide now. We must go."

"Mates or not, I'm still my own person," Sarai protested. "I'm going."

Niall battled needing to keep her safe with wanting to accede to her wishes. She was right about nowhere being protected anymore, though. At least this way, she'd be next to him where he could keep a close eye on her.

He extended a hand. "Come on, then. You're a staunch asset in battle. I'd welcome your presence."

"Thank you." A smile illuminated her face.

Stephan ran back the way he'd come, with Niall

and Sarai right behind him. As soon as they cleared the buildings, they joined a small group with magic bubbling around them.

"You're bringing a woman?" An eagle shifter shot a disapproving look Niall's way. Fair hair hung to his shoulders, and he had a pair of shrewd dark eyes.

"She's my mate," Niall replied. "She's coming with us."

The eagle snorted. "Mate, eh. Deucedly poor timing for new mate bonds, but whatever. Join the circle. We were waiting for you to launch our travel spell."

Niall wrapped a protective arm around Sarai. He was enough of a control freak, he hated trusting anyone else's magic, but he didn't know where to find Micah. Apparently, the eagle shifter did.

"Ready, mate," he said, tightlipped. "First stop has to be my car to parcel out what I have for weapons."

"I assume you're parked where the road went to crap?" The eagle shifter sent a sharp look, reminiscent of the raptor he turned into, Niall's way.

"Aye. You'd be correct. In fact, since we all know where it is, let's get there on our own, and we can save the group grope for once we're armed."

Without waiting for assents—or disagreement—he draped a spell around himself and Sarai, transporting them the few miles to where he'd left the Toyota. Stephan was right behind them.

"What's wrong? You don't trust them." Sarai spoke low, right against his ear.

"Never been the trusting sort," Niall agreed and popped the trunk latch. He did not want to go into detail on all the ways group spells could go wrong. They were easier to derail than individual castings, and he was certain vampires—fueled by mage power—would be expecting the cavalry to show up in full bloom.

He unwrapped the moldy leather and grabbed the saber he'd used, handing another to Stephan. It left one other saber, the fencing foil, and the two hunting knives. And the wooden box.

Niall opened it and drew out a clear fire opal suspended from a thick, golden chain. He draped it over Sarai's head, and the pendant nestled between her breasts, looking as if it belonged there. The colors flashed warmly.

"I love you, darling. If I'm still alive, I'll tell you the history behind the opal. There's a ring and bracelet as well, but they'd be in the way in a fight."

She smiled tightly. "You have to remain alive. Death isn't an option. Not now that we've discovered each other. Erm, I'm delighted with the gift, but how about one of those knives?"

"A practical wench. I love it." He moved aside. She chose an ivory-handled knife with an eight-inch serrated blade attached to a sheath that she tied around her waist with a leather cord.

The other four men arrived, deciding who'd take the saber and who got the other hunting knife and fencing blade. It left Jeremiah without a weapon, but he said, "It's all right. Mages truly are not fighters. I've never fought with a blade—or fought much at all, to be honest."

"Are you certain you want to come with us?" Niall asked, concern pricking him.

Jeremiah nodded tightly. "Yes. Vampires stole power from my kin. I need to be there. Maybe I can talk sense into mages who've allowed themselves to be drafted by evil."

"Words can be potent weapons, son." Stephan clapped Jeremiah on the back and told the eagle shifter, "We're good to go, man. Let's hit it."

Niall closed the Toyota's trunk and threaded an arm around Sarai. The gemstone, and its companion pieces still in the oak box, had been in the MacLier family for at least a thousand years. They went to the mate of the pack alpha, but shifters had left their pack structure behind after moving to the States. Niall would have been the alpha in charge of all varieties of cat shifter, but such conventions didn't matter anymore.

It was why he'd come close to giving the jewelry away, but he was glad he'd hung onto it. Even if no one needed alphas any longer, the gems would add an additional layer of protection for Sarai, intensifying her magic and making her a stronger fighter.

The opal was already bonding to her. He felt a subtle alteration in the warp and weft of its emanations. Sarai leaned into his side as the travel magic snared them. Niall kicked himself for not asking how far they were going. They'd get there when they got there, but still, he liked to have an idea of how long it should take.

That way he'd have a warning if something diverted them from their chosen trajectory.

"You're worried." Sarai employed telepathy since normal speech wasn't possible during travel spells. It disturbed the energy enough to sometimes deactivate them entirely.

"I'd be a fool not to be," he countered. *"Make no mistake, we'll be in the thick of it as soon as this casting disperses."*

"Try not to worry about me. I don't want you to get yourself killed because you weren't paying attention to defending yourself." Even in telepathy, her words were fierce.

"And I'd tell you the same, darling."

He waited until it felt like too much time had elapsed. Just as he was about to pull the plug on the threads holding himself and Sarai to the group's magic, the casting developed an insubstantial aspect. They were nearly at their destination.

"Soon," he said.

"I know. I felt the change too," she replied.

Mist surrounded them as they rolled out atop an Aubusson rug. Niall surged to his feet, dragging Sarai upright along with him and drew power to cut through the fog making it impossible to see.

Once it cleared, he was almost sorry he'd been in such a hurry. An enormous room that looked more like it belonged in a manor house or castle than somewhere in the States formed. Beams crisscrossed high above him, and a fireplace tall enough to accommodate an ox for roasting took up one end of the room.

"Where are we?" Sarai asked.

The air glittered wetly. Vampires came into view, one after the other, until at least twenty surrounded their small group. One stepped forward and engaged in a parody of a bow. White silk robes sashed in red fell around him, doing little to conceal his perfect form. Golden curls framed his patrician features.

How could they be so beautiful—and so rotten-to-the-core evil?

"Welcome to my home," the vampire purred. "I do hope you'll decide to remain. Adding shifter magic to our own is the next step in our experiment. I'll ask that you toss your weapons into the center of the room. It's not polite to bring sabers inside."

Niall threw his blade a few feet away. Close enough he could retrieve it in a pinch. He hoped. The vampire stalked to the other two shifters clutching swords and pried them loose, adding them to the pile. He didn't seem to sense the hunting knives.

Out of sight, out of mind. Good to know. Niall filed the information away.

The vampire transferred his obsidian gaze to Jeremiah. "Nicely done, my lad. Step forward and claim your reward."

Offering them a withering gaze over on shoulder, Jeremiah sauntered to the vampire and presented his neck for feeding.

Fury roared through Niall, but he needed a cool head. How the hell had Jeremiah managed to divert their travel spell to Castle Vampire? A quick glance at the four shifters yielded an answer. All had the glassy-eyed look that meant they'd been hypnotized.

Sarai cast a surreptitious look his way from beneath lowered lids and slipped the opal under her top. The gem glowed with an angry light, and Niall understood it was what saved them from Jeremiah's trickery.

Stephan shook himself, his glazed appearance falling away. "Where the fuck are we?" he boomed.

"Jeremiah sold us out." Sarai's tone was flat.

Stephan narrowed his eyes and scanned the room. When he saw Jeremiah in thrall to the vampire, he set his jaw in a harsh line but didn't make a move toward him. No doubt, he'd absorbed the vampire host, hanging about like a flock of beautiful, deadly birds with their variously colored robes.

Niall stuffed his fisted hands into his pockets. The other three shifters would come around eventually. Once they did, he'd figure something out. Had the whole story about Micah been nothing but fabrication?

Likely, since Jeremiah had been the messenger.

Niall forced a neutral expression. He'd get to the bottom of this, and when he did, heads would roll.

CHAPTER 8

Sarai kept her eyes downcast. Danger lay in looking directly at the vampires, and she needed to think. As a mage, Jeremiah's magic was similar enough to theirs, he'd found a way to splice into the eagle shifter's travel spell. Even so, it was a bold move. He must have been confident he wouldn't be caught.

Had everything the mages said been lies? Were all of them part and parcel of the vampires' bid for what was looking a whole lot like world domination?

Heat pulsed from the opal. Clearly, it had its own magic, but why hadn't Niall mentioned it? Maybe because there hadn't been time. Or it might have been a path only she could tread. Some magics were gender-specific.

She stole a glance at Niall and rearranged her

jacket as a cover for moving the gemstone out of sight. So far, the vampires hadn't noticed it—at least she didn't think they had.

Sarai did a nose count, coming up with twenty-one vampires. She swallowed around a dry-as-dust throat, not liking their odds. Six of them against better than triple their numbers.

I can't think like that. If I do, fear will take over and I won't be worth a shit.

Around her, the other shifters were shaking off the effects of whatever perverted magic Jeremiah had drugged them with. Fury rolled from them in dull red waves once understanding sank in, but no one was stupid enough to wage a one-man war.

The vamps lounged, moving about the room and chatting with one another. Even though they were lowkey about it, Sarai felt their attention and their readiness to strike if any of the shifters so much as thought about launching a counter-attack.

She knew the feel of vampire magic now.

It made her skin crawl with its prickly heat and dead-things stench. They could cover up their reek, but they weren't bothering to. Why should they? Dinner was already here.

What had the vampire feeding from Jeremiah said? That shifters were the next link in the chain.

"I do not think so," her wolf muttered. *"We're nobody's pawns."*

"Do you see a way out of this?" she asked and waited, hoping the vampires hadn't heard her question. She could sense shifter magic when bond animals talked, but the vamps in the cabin hadn't been able to.

After two long breaths, she figured she'd been right about the vampires not hearing her—or her wolf. *"Well, do you?"* she repeated, anxious for ideas.

"Maybe."

While she waited for her bondmate to say more, she scanned the room. It was enormous, perhaps fifty feet long and half that wide. The ceiling soared a good twelve feet above her head, reinforced with beefy beams. Lush wall hangings, metal sculptures, and paintings lined the walls. The floor was rough wooden planks mostly covered by an Oriental rug she supposed was worth millions given its size and thickness. Only thing missing was windows, but it made perfect sense. Daylight was a showstopper for these fuckers, at least it had been before they'd sullied mage power, tacking it onto their own in some unknown fashion.

The vampire was done with Jeremiah. With a vacuous smile on his face, the mage walked to another vampire who bent to take a few swallows. From there, Jeremiah offered himself to a third, a fourth, and a fifth. None of them took more than a few token swigs.

Sarai was confused. The vamp who'd spoken with them had drunk for at least five minutes. Had the others already eaten. Was that why they didn't feed as long? She suppressed a shudder, not wanting to give them any indication they were getting to her. The whole blood-drinking thing was so unnatural it gave her the creeps.

Or maybe it was their total lack of concern for the natural world. If they could turn it into their own personal fountain, they'd do it in the space between two heartbeats. Not that they either breathed or had beating hearts.

Jeremiah had worked his way through half the room. He was weaving now, as if the various vamps had taken too much blood from him, but he doggedly marched to another who latched on.

"He's up to something," the wolf said.

She'd been thinking the same thing, but other than suicide by vampire, she'd be damned if she could figure it out.

Niall edged closer to her and clasped her hand, keeping his low and between them. She understood. The physical link might mean their telepathy would go unnoticed. *"Be ready."* He barely breathed the words into her mind.

She wanted to scream, "For what?" but squeezed his hand to let him know she understood.

Jeremiah had made the rounds of all but two of the vampires. He swayed and went to his knees. A vampire hooked an arm around him and deposited him on a sofa, offering something thick, dark red, and nauseating looking in a glass. Jeremiah ignored him and dropped his head back. His eyes fluttered shut with dark rings inscribed beneath them that hadn't been there before.

Sarai had kept her power shuttered, but she snaked a tendril of magic outward until it wrapped around Jeremiah. She had to find out what was going on here. The jagged bite of poison ricocheted back at her, and she would have stumbled if Niall weren't holding onto her.

She still didn't get it. Had the vamps poisoned the mage? Why would they do that?

The first vampire, the one who'd taken his sweet time feeding uttered a cry. His body began to smoke, skin sloughing off it in long, nauseating strips.

The world shifted on its axis, and Sarai understood. The poison had originated from the mage. It was why he'd kept going, presenting his neck to one vamp after the next until he couldn't walk anymore.

Niall leapt forward, snatching up the saber on top of the heap. Stephan snapped up the next one, and the eagle shifter the fencing foil. The other shifter, a wolf like her, pulled one of the hunting knives from a thigh sheath. The men jumped into the fray.

Not all the vampires were in as bad a shape as the first one, but then they hadn't drunk as much poison. Maybe they'd sensed something—or more likely they looked at mages much the same way she viewed vampires. As hideous manifestations not worth their time.

Niall swung the blade, beheading the nearest vampire amid a shower of black, stinking ichor. Stephan caught two standing side by side. He kept the blade moving until both heads lolled on the priceless carpet, staining its intricate pattern beyond recognition.

Sarai yanked her knife free. The opal burned against her skin, and she instinctively linked her magic to it. Power surged through her, and she plunged the blade into the nearest vampire, not expecting to kill it—only beheading would to that—but she could damn good and sure immobilize it for one of the men to do away with.

The two vampires who hadn't fed from Jeremiah were edging toward a door at the end of the big room. They'd shrouded themselves, but it didn't fool her. She shifted, clothing shredding around her and the golden necklace still in place around her wolf's neck as she ran for the fucking no-good cowardly vampires who thought they could escape.

Oh hell no, not on her watch, they wouldn't.

She leapt on one, growling and snarling, and closed her fangs around its neck, biting hard. The nasty, bitter taste revolted her, but she didn't stop to spit it out.

Motion next to her turned out to be Stephan, blade swinging in an arc as he beheaded the other would-be escapee.

"Let go," Stephan told her.

She jumped away from the downed vampire, spitting out blood and hair. Stephan brought the blade down in a two-handed maneuver that neatly severed its head.

Panting, sides heaving, she surveyed the room. Five vampires were still on their feet, but their smoking bodies didn't pose much of a threat. Her gaze fell on Jeremiah, still collapsed in the same chair.

His face was white, his breathing labored. Clearly, the deadly substance he'd ingested was killing him too. After thanking her wolf for its valor, she summoned magic to shift back to human and threaded her way through vampire remains in various stages of decomposition until she reached him.

Sarai clasped his hand. "Jeremiah."

His blue eyes fluttered open, and he offered a ghost of a smile. "Tell Chloe it worked and that I love her."

Sarai's eyes rounded in surprise. "She knew."

"T-they all did." He made a gagging sound.

She looked around for water but didn't see any. "Why did you do this?"

He closed his eyes as if keeping them open took too much effort.

Niall crouched next to her. "What can I do?"

"Look for some water for him." Sarai turned back to Jeremiah. If she was any judge, death hovered close by.

He blew out a breath, followed by bubbles of blood-tinged saliva. "We set this up to warn mages aligned with evil. They will sense what I have done, know mages are behind..." His words disappeared in a coughing fit. Blood flowed freely out of his mouth.

"It's all right." She tightened her hold on his hand. "I understand. Other mages will take this as a warning not to parlay with vampires."

He nodded.

Niall returned with a carafe of water and held it to Jeremiah's lips. He tried to swallow but coughed most of it back out. Sarai took the jug and tipped some water into her mouth, swishing it around and spitting it out to rid her mouth of vampire residue. She thought twice before spitting on the carpet, but it was such a godawful mess, one more mouthful of anything wouldn't make a whit of difference.

The eagle shifter ran to them and placed his hands on either side of Jeremiah's head. Sarai felt a jolt of magic and figured the eagle must command healing magic. She could do simple things, but Jeremiah's problem was beyond her skills.

Jeremiah cracked his eyes again. "Let me go," he said to the eagle shifter. "Too far gone."

"You are not." The eagle's tone cracked like a whip. "Are you going to help me or feel so sorry for yourself you give up?"

"I will help." More blood gushed, this time from nose and mouth, running down his chest. "Hurts," he moaned. "Burns."

Sarai didn't see how the eagle shifter could intervene. The death she'd sensed earlier was indeed close.

"Give me room to work," the eagle instructed.

Sarai let go of Jeremiah's hand. "I'll be here," she told him. "I'm not going anywhere."

Niall led her to a small table where a pile of clothing sat. "While I was on the prowl for water, I poked through a closet or two. Didn't figure you'd want a vampire robe, but these bastards made a practice of imprisoning human slaves to feed from. They had quite a clothing collection."

"Did you free who you found?"

"Aye. Those who weren't too debilitated have already left." Niall didn't mention the others, and she didn't ask not wanting any more of a visual than she already had.

Sarai picked through the stack, finding woolen pants, a stretchy top, and a tightly woven sweater. Niall had even come up with socks. "Thanks. Want to help me find my shoes?"

"Where are they?"

She pointed to where she'd been standing when she'd seen the vampires heading for freedom. Niall kicked vampire bones aside, digging until he came up with first one running shoe, and then the other.

Shoes always survived shifting. She put them on about the time a pitiful howl rose from Jeremiah. Her eyes filled with tears when she looked at Niall. "Damn but he was brave."

"Aye, but he used us. Lied to us."

"True enough, but if we'd known, he probably couldn't have pulled this off. One of the vamps might have picked up the plot from our minds."

Niall wrapped his arms around her. "Darling, the road to hell is paved with good intentions."

"You're quoting proverbs?"

He smiled. "Is that what it is. I've always credited Saint Bernard of Clairvaux with that one."

She rolled her eyes. "When did he live?"

Niall shrugged. "Middle of the twelfth century, give or take."

Another gut-wrenching shriek filled the room. Stephan joined them. "We need to leave. I've ascertained we're in Eastern Europe. It will take a long time—and a lot of magic—to get back to the ghost town where we left everyone."

"That would explain the castle," Niall muttered.

The harsh astringent smell of poison grew far stronger. Sarai worked her way around pools of ichor and vampire remains to return to Jeremiah. It felt like she'd abandoned him to the torments of the damned.

The eagle shifter sat next to the mage, hunting knife in hand, chanting in Gaelic. He'd stripped off Jeremiah's clothing and made a series of ritualistic cuts along his torso, inner arms, and inner thighs. Whenever he hit a certain note, all the cuts pulsed, and clear liquid oozed from them.

Sarai looked closely at the mage's face. It didn't appear quite so pasty and drawn, and he was breathing a little better. She hadn't believed the eagle shifter, but damn if his intervention wasn't working.

Stephan knelt next to the eagle. "Ronnie. How much longer?"

"I'm almost done. We have to get moving, huh?"

"Is Jeremiah strong enough for a long teleport?" Sarai asked, concerned about the mage who'd decided to play double agent, with foreknowledge he'd pay the ultimate price for his valor.

"I think so," the eagle replied. "He's tough. I wasn't sure I could stop the poison's spread, but once we got going, things went better than I expected."

Niall and the wolf shifter joined them.

The eagle sang one more round of chanting. This time, barely anything extruded from the cuts. "Good enough," the eagle muttered. He placed his hand atop each of the wounds, and they closed as if they'd never been there.

Groaning, Jeremiah rolled to a sit, and the healer helped him with his clothes. Jeremiah made a face. "Ewww. I stink like vampires."

"We all do, son," the eagle said. "Welcome back from death's doorstep."

"Thanks for not giving up on me." The mage smiled crookedly but winced as he slid his jacket over his shoulders.

The eagle shifter made a face. "I work as hard as my patients. If you'd told me you were finished, that you'd given up, I'd have had second thoughts about stepping in."

Niall planted himself in front of Jeremiah. "Was the tale about Micah false?" At Jeremiah's nod, he continued. "How could you be sure he wouldn't return and spoil everything for you?"

Jeremiah focused bloodshot blue eyes on Niall. "I wasn't. It was the only part of tonight that was a calculated guess. I assumed if we moved quickly enough, none of the ones who'd gone for weapons would be back."

Niall bent so he was nose to nose with Jeremiah. Sarai felt the bite of a truth spell. "Was Micah in on this?"

"No. We would never have put a shifter in the position of choosing loyalty to his people over helping us." The mage's words vibrated with the ring of truth, even absent Niall's casting.

Niall straightened. "I'll manage the travel spell this time." His voice didn't give anything away, but Sarai suspected he was still angry at being lied to and used. Never mind, the mage had a higher purpose. There were a whole lot of junctures where his strategy could have gone off the rails.

She had questions too, but they could wait.

The familiar feel of Niall's magic rose around her. This time, the opal thrummed in time to his spell, perfectly attuned to MacLier power. Stephan and the eagle shifter supported Jeremiah between them. He protested he could stand on his own, but they blanketed him in a shroud of healing magic.

The walls of the vampires' lair first thinned and then faded entirely. Sarai sucked a breath deep into her lungs, enjoying the taste and feel of air that wasn't tainted by rot. The return trip didn't seem to take as long, but she was exhausted and not tracking well. Three vampire confrontations in two days would drain anyone.

"*When did you know about Jeremiah?*" she asked her bondmate.

"*I sensed the poison from the first vampire but wasn't sure until the third.*"

"*Why didn't you tell me?*"

The wolf chuffed. "*Because I didn't know whether they could hear us. This group was old, powerful. They may have had different abilities than the ones in the cabin. Anyway, they were engaged in doing their typical vamp thing. Never turn down blood when its offered. I saw no reason to interrupt them.*"

"*How do you know so much about vampires?*" Sarai was curious. The shifter bond was an interesting phenomenon, one where the animal knew everything about her, but she knew next to nothing about it.

"*They were common as rats in earlier times. You're far from my first bondmate.*"

"*Sometime, you'll have to tell me more.*"

"*Maybe someday I will, but my history isn't important, only our bond is.*"

Niall's magic lulled her, and it was a struggle not to give up and close her eyes. The teleport spell would unfold even with her unconscious, but after everything that had transpired, she didn't see how she could check out. If one travel spell could be diverted, another could too.

Niall brought them down on the outskirts of Golddust. The mages—all of whom had known what Jeremiah was up to—raced to them, their eyes full of questions.

When Chloe saw Jeremiah, she threw herself into his arms and gasped. "But you're still alive. How it that possible?"

He hugged his sister. "Shifters are nothing if not determined. No wonder we lost that war." He let go of Chloe and clasped hands with the other mages, assuring them the deed was done.

The mages' heartfelt reunion warmed Sarai. She remained until she was weaving on her feet then went hunting for Niall, intent on determining where they'd sleep for a few hours. Because it was the path of least resistance, she sent magic spinning outward, seeking him.

He was in the deserted saloon with most of the shifters, none of whom looked particularly happy. Fury streamed from Micah at being exploited to trick his kinsmen into taking an enormous risk.

Her head might be fuzzy, but she couldn't figure out what was wrong. They'd struck a significant blow tonight, killed enough vampires to make a difference.

"Sarai." Niall's summons held gruff edges.

She trudged to his side, beyond tired. "What's up? I need sleep."

"We all do, but this meeting was essential. We'll be severing all ties with the mages. We cannot trust them."

She fell back a step. "What?"

"I was clear enough."

"Well, it's a mistake. Jeremiah was a hero. He would have died to set an example to other mages."

"I know all that, but you cannot stand next to a man you cannot trust."

Her temper, always short-fused, flared. "That's a bunch of medieval twaddle. He did the best he could." She spread her hands in front of her. "We had success—"

"Aye, we got lucky. There are untold numbers of ways his half-baked plan could have gone sideways, and then we'd all have ended up vampire fodder."

"But—"

"Enough. The point isn't up for discussion."

The opal grew warm where it nested between her breasts. Was it warning her or egging her on? Sarai didn't care. "It was 'up for discussion' before I got here. Besides, you can't tell me what to do or how to think."

"Not trying to—"

"The hell you aren't." She spun and raced out of the dilapidated building, not sure where she'd go, but planning to put as much distance as she could between herself and Niall.

Her magical reservoir was mostly untouched. All she'd done lately was shift. She heard Niall calling her name and ran the other way, summoning a teleport spell to take her back to her shop. It needed cleaning, and at least that would divert her attention from the old-fashioned prig he'd turned into.

Nah. He didn't turn into anything. It's what he's always been.

Tears leaked from her eyes as the magic took her. She blinked them away and ground her teeth until her jaws ached. Niall was a selfish, narrow-minded bastard, and she hoped to hell she never saw him again.

Ever.

If she could get herself to buy into that, she'd be golden. Breath hissed through her clenched teeth. The opal throbbed between her breasts, singing its own melody. She was new to its energy and had no idea what it was trying to tell her, but she needed to get rid of it too. In case it had some underhanded way of driving her back into Niall's arms.

CHAPTER 9

*N*iall grabbed his favorite saber from the pile where the men had tossed their weapons and pounded out of the saloon, running after Sarai. She had a head start, though, and fury added speed to her flight. Magic flared fifty yards to the south as she engaged a travel spell, and he skidded to a halt.

Damned reactive woman. What was wrong with her?

Stephan caught up with him. "She left, eh?"

"Aye. Is she always this volatile?" Words spewed before Stephan could answer. "We made our decision, a quorum of us, the way 'tis always been done. How could she question our wisdom? It exists to protect her and all the rest of us too."

Stephan stood in the dark street, quiet and watchful.

"Well?" Niall demanded. "She's your kin. Shed some light on her behavior. It's unacceptable for her not to accept my guidance. She knows less than nothing about—"

Stephan held up a hand. "Listen to yourself, man. So far, you've said Sarai is weak and incapable of thinking for herself."

"I have not," Niall sputtered.

"Then we have nothing more to discuss." Stephan dropped his hand and turned to walk away.

Niall grabbed his upper arm. "Aye, we do. She's my mate."

Stephan jerked out of his grip and spun to face him. The mountain cat shifter narrowed his eyes. "Maybe you haven't paid attention, but the world is a different place than it was when you and I came into it. Marie was old, like me, so we played by the original rulebook. It created friction when Sarai came to live with us, but we came to respect and appreciate her approach to most things. Not everything, mind you, but she brought a freshness to our household and pushed us to embrace women's innate strength and instinctual knowledge.

"It may be hard for you to understand this, but Marie blossomed—came into her own in ways I'd never have predicted—after a few years with Sarai beneath our roof."

Niall shook his head. Stephan was spouting words, but they weren't making a whole lot of sense. "Can you distill that into something simpler?"

"Sure. You have to give Sarai an equal seat at the table. I heard what she said in the saloon. She believes Jeremiah was a hero. You see him as a traitor." Stephan paused for emphasis. "You're going to have to meet her halfway. The flip side of that coin is she's going to have to want to bridge the gap between you. Sarai has always had a hot temper. She may have written you off as a chauvinistic cad."

"She can't do that. She's my mate. Mine." Outrage laced with possessiveness beat a path through Niall.

"Uh-huh. There's another problem. She will never see herself as your property. Think about it before you chase after her. If you find her in your current state of mind—and the mate bond will accomplish that—you'll only make things worse."

The air took on a glistening aspect as Stephan called power.

"Where are you going?" Niall asked.

"Home. Sarai may be there, but I wouldn't bet on it. I'm tired, and I want to mourn the loss of my mate."

Remorse cut deep. Niall had been so immersed in his own anger and worries, he'd all but forgotten about the other man's loss. He bowed his head. "Thank you for everything you did after your mate's death. I am so sorry I never got to meet her. She must have been a very special woman."

A sad smile flitted about Stephan's mouth. "Marie was amazing. The best. So's Sarai—if you accept her for who she is and don't try to twist her into some female ideal you crafted back in the sixteen hundreds." The magic brightened around him. When it cleared, Niall was alone.

He stuffed one hand into a pocket and set off at a quick pace, heading toward where he'd left his car. The saber was heavy, awkward, and he wished for a scabbard across his back. The sky was growing lighter to his left with the breaking dawn. Any other day, he'd have appreciated the pearlescent aspect as black shaded to a pinkish-gray. The evening star hung low on the horizon almost as if it were keeping an eye on him.

What should he do?

Go after her or give her time to think through her folly?

He winced and ran faster. If Stephan was to be believed, Sarai didn't view the stand she'd taken as folly. She wasn't trying to be contrary or test him; she truly believed Jeremiah had done a brave and noble thing.

Why couldn't she see it from his point of view?

A cross between a snort and a growl rolled from his

mouth. Stephan had addressed that too, and quite succinctly when he'd said Niall had to meet her halfway.

His jaguar had been uncharacteristically quiet. "Are you going to tell me what you think?" he queried his bondmate.

"Do you really want to know?"

Something about the cat's tone gave him pause. "Aye, or I'd not have asked."

"You won't like most of what I have to say."

"Oh for fuck's sake get on with it." He shifted the blade to his other hand and kept on running.

"When you chose to remain single, I mourned because I wished for us to have a mate, but you have never treated your bed partners very well. Over time, I came to recognize the wisdom in your choice to remain by yourself."

"What do you mean, I haven't treated them well?" Niall bristled. "I've always been honest with them about who I am and what I could give."

"That's precisely it. You never gave them much more than your cock. If any of them began to care about you, you cut them out of your life."

"I know all those things. What I fail to see is how they're relevant to Sarai's temperamental outburst."

"Listen to yourself. She felt strongly enough about

something to stand up to you. Rather than respecting her opinion, you labeled it hysteria." The jaguar kept right on rolling. *"Until you accept—and pay heed to—what's important to her, you'll never be much of a mate. Or a man, I might add."*

Niall was sorry he'd asked, but the jaguar had warned him. His bondmate fell silent, clearly done with talking.

The outlines of cars loomed ahead, surprising him. Either he was faster than he thought, or he'd been running for a longer time. Some of the vehicles had left, which was the plan they'd agreed to. Everyone was going home for a few days where they'd lie low and assess if the mages' plot changed things, or if the vampire attacks would keep right on rolling. Niall had left before Micah scared up the mages and delivered the message they wouldn't be working together from here on in. He wondered how that had gone. If it weren't for Jeremiah's kamikaze act, he'd have pegged the mages for a bunch of second-rate magic wielders.

He scrunched his face into a grimace. He'd come to that conclusion long before they lost the war and never bothered to revisit it. Maybe he really was a bigoted bastard. Just because mage magic couldn't secure a shifter bond didn't mean it was an inferior brand of power.

Jeremiah had been plenty strong enough to co-opt the eagle shifter's travel spell.

A wave of discomfort rolled through him, followed by another. He wasn't used to facing his feelings, and he understood why. Acknowledging he was—er, might be—wrong dumped him into a squirmy awkward spot where it was damned hard to keep on keeping on.

He'd planned to move Sarai into his house and go back to work. He hadn't discussed it with her. She was his mate. He'd assumed she'd agree, but maybe not. He did live in a pretty sketchy section of a town three hours from her shop.

Aye, I assumed she'd walk away from her life and shape herself to fit into mine.

He sucked in a tight breath and opened his trunk to toss the saber inside. The wooden box caught his eye, and he picked it up, springing the catch. The opal ring and bracelet caught rays of the rising sun, reflecting them in myriad colors. He closed the intricately carved box but kept it with him. Regardless of how things went, she deserved the companion jewelry to her pendant, and he'd see she had them.

He'd been selfish and a fool.

How could he have misjudged so badly?

Because I've always been at the center of my own universe.

The answer was sobering—and enlightening.

Maybe it wasn't too late to set things right with Sarai. Her uncle said she had a hot temper. Maybe she'd cooled down enough to at least hear him out.

He got behind the wheel, intent on driving back to Denver and her shop. It wasn't far. Shouldn't take him more than an hour, and he could stop at a café and bring her breakfast. Maybe he'd stop at a hardware store and buy cleaning supplies too. Her shop had been trashed, but he was almost certain she'd go there rather than Stephan and Marie's.

The shop was hers, and she was wounded so she'd want to go to ground in a place she was unlikely to be disturbed.

Aye, and the reason she's wounded is because of me. No need to sugarcoat it.

Niall swallowed, the taste of bitterness and defeat coating his tongue. Once he was a little closer, he'd check her location through the mate bond. Undeterred by her dismissal, it vibrated just beneath his breastbone, mocking him but offering hope as well.

The mate bond was the goddess's gift to those like him. It ensured loyalty and continuation of their magical species. Sarai would sense it just as intensely as he did. He pounded a fist on the steering wheel. She had to hear him out. He'd apologize, do whatever it took to get them back on an even keel.

Love laced with deep longing for her poured

through him and made him realize how empty his life had been. He peeled back layers as he drove, not sparing any quarter as he picked through the emotional wasteland his life had been. He'd always known he was an adrenaline junkie who craved anything so long as it was new and unusual. What he hadn't realized was how jumping from fighting one fire to the next had stunted his ability to relate to people.

Mostly, he'd clumped them into categories, never bothering to dig any deeper once he assigned a label. His tags for women had been simple. They'd either been potential sex partners—or not.

He swallowed hard, not caring much for his in-depth moral inventory, but if he was going to bare his soul to Sarai, he needed to view himself from an objective position. No matter how much it pained him.

And he needed to tell her everything. Come clean.

Not that he planned to grovel—it wasn't in his nature—but he would do his damnedest to work with her and offer her his full attention. He'd listen to what she had to say and hunt for how they could craft compromises. He vowed to never tell her she was wrong, or that she had to view the world through his lens.

He reached the exit for her shop and sent a thread of magic snaking outward to make certain he'd guessed right about her location.

She was indeed there, and it set off a cascade of conflicting reactions. So much so, he longed for the safe cocoon he'd shrouded himself in for so long. He was pleased he'd guessed right, but maybe that had been all mate bond and not him at all.

Aye, lesson number two. Watch what I take credit for.

Apprehension tightened his throat and tied his stomach into a knot. What if she wouldn't let him in? What would he do then? How would he talk with her if she'd decided he was too big a mouthful of diehard chauvinist to bother with?

He'd tightened his fingers around the wheel until his hands cramped, and he made a conscious effort to relax them. He had to believe all wasn't lost. He nosed the Toyota into a slightly closer parking spot than he'd had last time and got out of the car, ducking back inside to snatch up the wooden box. A coffee shop sat across the street from him, and he sprinted to it, intent on buying coffee and muffins or whatever they had that looked decent.

Remembering his thoughts about cleaning supplies, he glanced up and down the street. A corner market in her office building would probably have bleach and ammonia and sponges and paper towels. He ducked into the small café. It smelled delicious. Cinnamon, vanilla, coffee, and caramel blended into an assault on his empty belly. He couldn't remember the last time he'd eaten, which wasn't good. Magic was like any other physical process. It required fuel and sleep to function at its best.

He strode to the counter and bought two large coffees. He started to tell the clerk to add sugar and cream to both but stopped himself. He had her make up one the way he liked it and got sugar and cream to go for Sarai. For all he knew, she preferred her brew black.

"Anything else, sir?" The clerk, a young redhead with huge gray eyes gave him a definite come-on look.

Normally, he'd have flirted with her, testing the waters and making a date for when she got off shift, but no more. He was a mated man, even if his mate might be done with him.

"Aye, I'll take four of those iced scones, two cinnamon buns, and two of those ham and cheese croissants."

"Ooooh, I simply adore British accents," she gushed as she dropped the items he'd selected into white bags.

Yup. He'd pegged it right when she batted her eyelashes his way. He gathered the snacks and coffees in a carry container and dropped a twenty on the glass-topped counter. "Keep the change, and I'm Irish."

"So? It's right next door, yes?" She smiled and drew her tongue over her upper lip in obvious invitation.

Niall didn't waste time telling her no self-respecting Irishman took being mistaken for a Brit lying down. He shouldered out the door, feeling the heat of her gaze following him. The old Niall would have been all over her no-strings fuck-me vibes, but he hadn't even been marginally tempted.

Maybe there was hope for him, after all.

A quarter hour later, laden with bags of cleaning supplies and food from the café, he punched the elevator button and rode the car down to Sarai's floor. The journey to the end of the corridor took forever and was over in the blink of an eye. Because his hands were full, he tapped the door with a foot.

Time dribbled past. He felt her energy and was certain she knew he was there. He'd just raised his foot to tap the door again when she called, "Go away."

Niall was damned if he'd turn tail and run just because she told him to. He may have finally faced his failings, but he'd never been one to walk away from something he wanted.

And he wanted Sarai more than life itself.

Without thinking through the ramifications, or he might not have done it, he focused a jot of magic. The door *snicked* open, and he walked through. Sarai was on her hands and knees with a scrub brush and a bucket of red-tinged water. Her face was blotchy, and he was certain she'd been crying.

Her tears broke his heart but gave him faith it wasn't too late for them. He set down his burdens. "I brought more cleaning stuff, and coffee and pastries. This coffee is yours. If you want cream and sugar, they're in the small bag."

Before she could do more than gape at him, he snatched up the bucket of filthy water. "I'll just run this down to the men's room and fill it with fresh. Back in a flash."

Niall located a janitorial closet before he found the men's room. It had a floor drain and spigots, so he dumped the water and cleaned the bucket before refilling it. So far so good. She hadn't yelled at him. Hadn't run toward him intent on ripping his eyes out. His arm brushed the lump the wooden box made in his jacket pocket. What with the food and market items, he'd almost forgotten the ring and bracelet.

Her door still stood ajar. He walked through and kicked it shut. She'd moved to a chair and was sipping coffee and clutching a mostly eaten cinnamon bun. He noted she'd added cream to her coffee and filed that fact away, along with a ripped open sugar packet lying on her desk.

There was a new Niall in town. A considerate man who noticed small things like how his mate liked her coffee. He set the bucket with clean water down and drew the wooden box from his pocket, placing it on a table.

"What's that?" she asked.

"The jewelry that goes with your pendant. They're yours," he hurried on, "no matter what happens between us."

A constellation of emotions played over her face, each one gone before he could decipher it. "Thank you for thinking of me." Her tone was oddly formal, and his gut lurched into his throat. "It was kind of you to bring me something to eat and more cleaning materials, but that doesn't change anything between us."

"But I was wrong," he said, anxious to get that out on the table.

She shook her head and put down her cup. "No. You were just being you. I'm a shifter too, remember? I've lived with our people my entire life, and I recognize how you old ones are. There're too many differences between you and me. It will never work. Not without a whole lot of friction that makes us both miserable."

He opened his mouth, but she held up a hand, palm outward. "Hear me out. The reason I didn't get more cleaning done was because I was doing some research. According to one of my sourcebooks, there is a way out of the mate bond. It's a simple enough ceremony, and it won't harm either of us—or our bond animals."

He pulled a chair until it faced her and dropped into it. "Is that what you really want?" He kept his words low, gentle.

"Yes. It's for the best." Her eyes sheened with tears. "Sorry. I can't stop crying. It will pass. It's three vampire confrontations and not enough to eat and my aunt dying and..." A sob obliterated her next words.

He wanted to surge forward and cradle her in his arms, but it would be a mistake. She'd accuse him of taking advantage of her in a weak moment. He also didn't mention that her flirting with uprooting their mate bond would tear her heart out, no matter what her reference book suggested.

"We will do whatever you want. I promise I won't pressure you, but I'd like it if you'd hear me out."

"I—I'm not sure that's wise," she snuffled. "You might snare me in some kind of spell."

Aye, darling. You're already snared in the mate bond. Sure and it's plenty strong without me adding aught to it.

Because she didn't tell him not to, he started talking, the words bubbling directly from his soul. She might still insist they dissolve their bond—if such a thing were even possible—but he wouldn't give her up without a fight. Without doing his damnedest to let her know how important she was to him.

And what a fool he'd been not to respect her interpretation of Jeremiah's bold and dangerous actions.

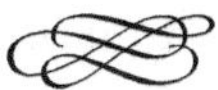

CHAPTER 10

Sarai blinked away tears, but more welled behind them. She had to pull herself together. What a weak suck bitch she was. Part of her had actually been thrilled to see Niall. So thrilled it was a struggle not to launch herself into his arms. She might be touched by his thoughtfulness, but she couldn't let herself be diverted by gestures. Nothing changed what he'd revealed about his character in the saloon in Golddust.

Nothing, and she had to hold that knowledge front and center.

Rather than a flood of reassurances he had no intention of catching her up in a spell, he said, "I would tell you a story, if you'll indulge me for a moment or two. It's not a tale I've told anyone. At the time it happened, I was truly young and deeply ashamed. I didn't realize my reaction to those events would shape my life. And not in ways I'm proud of."

"It's not necessary," she murmured, but she couldn't bring herself to tell him a flat-out no and chase him out of her shop.

What the fuck is wrong with me?

The opal warmed where it hung between her breasts, emitting soothing emanations almost as if it were urging her to listen. She should jerk the chain over her head and rid herself of the gem. It was linked to the MacLiers, so of course it would be on Niall's side. The gem thrummed hotly in clear disagreement with her plan, but it needn't have bothered. She couldn't divest herself of it anymore than she could tell Niall to piss up a rope and leave.

He leaned closer but stopped shy of touching her. "May I continue?"

Sarai nodded, not trusting what might come out of her mouth. Part of her didn't want him to share intimate secrets about trials that had shaped him, but a far bigger part wanted to soak in every single scrap of data about the jaguar shifter sitting a few inches away.

"Thank you. I appreciate it. This will not take long." His words were formal, old-fashioned, and they highlighted the centuries dividing them.

"While I'm certain you studied the war that drove us from the Old Country," he went on, "reading about it in books can't be anything like being there. I was sloppy, full of hubris, and not paying attention. A group of mages intent on separating me from my animal nature zeroed in on my brashness and abducted me. The world was a very different place then. The only method my kin would have had to track me was magic, and since the mages swathed me in spells, I was cut off from everyone and everything.

"They moved me to northern Scotland, sequestering me in a castle dungeon. The only person I saw for months was a comely maid who brought me a water bucket and occasional bits of food. Enough to keep me alive, but not much more.

"Since I had no other options, I began a slow process of luring her with magic. I saw in her eyes that she hated what was being done to me, but she was a very low-ranking mage and not able to pick and choose the tasks assigned to her."

Sarai licked dry lips. "This mage, what was her name?"

"Karina. I never knew her last name. She wasn't yet twenty, and she had a warm and lively spirit. Because I was lonely as well as desperate, my spell caught me up too. I came to crave the times when she'd stop for a while and talk with me."

Niall took a ragged breath. Sarai steeled herself. The harsh places in this tale were nearly upon her.

"We had months, Karina and I, to get to know one another. I never meant to, but I fell in love with her, and her visits progressed from kisses to making love. My jaguar warned me, told me what a wretchedly bad idea she and I were, but I didn't listen, and I should have. It would have saved me centuries of guilt.

"With her help, I hatched a plan to escape. She snuck me extra food to shore up my magic, and we picked a meeting place. Our intent was to run away together to a place no one knew us." A slow, sad breath hissed from between his teeth.

"She left the door to my cell unlocked, and so I left the dungeon. I lay low for two days and then went to the abbey where we were supposed to meet."

Niall's voice broke, and he swallowed hard. "A priest was there. It was hallowed ground, so despite his hatred and distrust for all things magical, he couldn't harm me."

Sarai's heart thudded hard. She had a feeling what Niall would say next, and pain for him arrowed into her.

"Karina had come to the abbey mortally wounded. The priest found her, hovering on the brink of death. Her father and brother knew I'd escaped, and it wasn't hard for them to link her to me being gone. Justice in those days was swift and grim. They employed magic to make certain her death would be painful, and that she'd last long enough to tell someone her tale.

"You see, the mages wanted me to know my escape signed her death warrant. Poor, innocent Karina must have told them we loved one another and were planning to run away together." He folded his hands in his lap so tightly, the knuckles turned white. "The priest took pity on me and showed me where he'd buried her in an unmarked grave outside the regular cemetery."

"It was kind of him."

"Not so much. She should have been cremated, just like us. Burying her sealed her in the in-between place where there is neither life nor death." He shook his head. "I loved her, and I used her, and she died because of me. Her only sin was falling in love with me, a process I encouraged."

He blew out a rough breath. "It was the last time I offered my heart to anyone. Until I met you." He untwined his hands and reached for one of hers. She gripped it, unable to refuse him. The amulet throbbed warmly.

"I was wrong back in Golddust. I shouldn't have discounted your feelings or your thoughts about Jeremiah. I am most truly sorry. I've never forgiven the mages for what they did to Karina, and it's colored my interactions with them ever since. I should have given

Jeremiah points for courage, but I was small-minded enough to aim for criticism instead." He stopped to take a measured breath. "I fanned the flames with the other shifters. If I'd taken a different tack, things could have gone another way. And I shall see that they do. We will rescind our ban on working with our mage cousins and ask them to forgive us. I suspect they'll understand."

Sarai gathered her thoughts. "It wasn't just Jeremiah. I saw how you do things. You and the men made a decision, and it was cast in stone. My father was much the same. Once he made up his mind, that was the end of it. Discussion closed. I never understood why my mother put up with him."

Niall laced his fingers with hers. She should pull her hand back but couldn't resist the feel of his skin against hers. "Your da, he wanted to keep you safe. You and the rest of his family. 'Tis the shifter way. We protect what's near and dear to us.

"With all the television and movie spotlights on paranormal phenomena and creatures, it's easy to get the idea people's tolerance for us has improved. Trust me, it hasn't. John Q. Citizen might love the idea of salting and burning bones on *Supernatural* or Jack the Ripper's diary coming alive on *Warehouse 13*, but faced with the reality of what we are, they'll run the other way."

He scooted his chair close enough their knees touched. "I took my shot at explaining to the priest about how I needed to exhume Karina so I could cremate her." Niall's nostrils flared with hatred. "You should have seen how he looked at me, with the holy fire of God in his eyes. I was an abomination. The reason men like him chose the priesthood. I told him I was going to see Karina had proper last rites—mine not his—and he jumped me."

"Bet that wasn't much of a contest," Sarai muttered.

"Nay, darling. It wasn't. I meant to knock him out so he'd stay out of my way for a few hours, but I hit him a wee bit too hard... At least I saw Karina's soul home to her ancestors, and then I fled. 'Twas a long journey back to Ireland since I didn't trust using magic—didn't want to draw attention to myself. By the time I showed up, the war was mostly over, and I joined my kin on the ship that brought us to the Americas."

Sarai chewed her lower lip. He'd given her a perfect opening, but if she told him her secrets, that would bring them closer, make it that much harder for her to hold to her stance they were done.

"Do the right thing," her wolf urged in its usual cryptic communication style.

The amulet sent a wave of affirmation into her breastbone.

Sarai rolled her eyes.

"What is it?" Niall drew his brows together. "Did my story disturb you?"

"Of course, but it's not that. My wolf is doing its Monday morning quarterback routine, and that damned amulet is like a miniature MacLier herding me."

Niall's mouth twitched. "Just wait until you add the ring and bracelet."

"Not sure I want to." She blew out a breath. "Oh hell. I know about humans being appalled by the reality of what we are."

"Oh? How might that be?"

She grinned crookedly. "I'm part of the generation that grew up watching *Supernatural* and *Vampire Diaries* and all those other shows about people like us. I thought they were cool, and that it was even cooler I had this gorgeous wolf as a bondmate. I was certain if I picked the right bunch of humans and shifted, they'd fawn all over me."

Niall winced. "Och, you didn't."

"'Fraid I did. And not just once. When the first batch screamed and scrambled and shit themselves, I figured I'd picked badly. So I did it again. And again. By then, my wolf form was all over the Internet. Everyone was convinced it was some kind of sophisticated parlor trick."

"Christ, darling. Your parents must have been devastated. And I'm shocked your wolf cooperated."

"My wolf almost broke our bond over my pranks." She winced at the memory. "Father and a bunch of the men blew through wads of magic wiping memories and computerized data bits. It was how I ended up with Stephan and Marie, who made it abundantly clear if I pulled any further shenanigans, they'd mute my magic as punishment."

"Did you?" He quirked a curious brow.

"No. By then, I was done. I'd run enough of an experiment to understand humans were a bunch of intolerant fuckers who talked a good game but weren't worth my time."

"I wasn't far off the mark with my assessment, then, was I?"

"No, it was surprisingly accurate." Sarai latched her gaze onto his, drawn by the warmth in his dark eyes. Warmth that could ignite into passion and silvery flecks—if she recanted from her stiff-necked attitude.

"For a Neanderthal?" The quirked brow edged up another notch.

Sarai couldn't help herself. She laughed.

"Does that mean you've forgiven me?"

"I guess it does. You're impossible to stay angry with."

He cast a knowing look her way. "Remember how I

said reading about the war isn't the same as living through it?" At her nod, he went on. "Well, reading about the mate bond isn't the same as being linked to another shifter through its magic. You may have come up with some formulaic mumbo-jumbo to end our bond, but those things never, ever work."

"How would you know? You've never been mated."

"It's a guess on my part, but the mate bond is sacred. It's a gift from the goddess to ensure the continuation of our kind. I cannot believe such a thing would disappear without an unholy struggle."

He got to his feet and drew her upright before folding his arms around her. She tucked her head into the hollow between his neck and shoulder feeling like she'd come home. He stroked her back with his big hands, leaving trails of heat in the wake of his fingertips.

"Thank you for not shutting the door on me." His deep voice rumbled near her ear. "Thank you for giving me a second chance. I promise to take better care of it—and of you."

She tilted her head back. "I'll hold you to it." Rising on her tiptoes, she kissed him, but only once. Before their passion could gain a toehold, she squirmed out of his embrace. "I want you, but so far we've made love in the dirt behind a rotting building. Maybe this time, we could aim for something softer?"

"Of course. Let's finish this cleaning project, and we can go anywhere you'd like including the fanciest hotel in Denver."

Happiness beat a track through her. "Gosh, I'd be happy with LaQuinta or a Motel 6. We can't very well go back to Stephan's. He might show up. Your house is too far away—unless we teleport." She was babbling, so she shut up.

Niall dropped the wooden box into her shoulder bag. "So you don't forget it." He dug into the plastic bags he'd piled in the corner and dragged out sponges and bleach. "I am not taking my brand-new mate to a cheap, chain motel. Pick something nice, or I'll decide for us."

She thought about it. "There's a Victorian bed and breakfast I've always thought was beautiful."

Niall fished out his cell phone. "Tell me the name, and I'll book us."

"Cora's Inn." She went back to work with the freshly filled bucket and scrub brush. Most of the large, colorful throw rug was as clean as she could get it, but black splotches remained. Maybe she should give up and order a new one. When she glanced up, Niall was standing in front of her computer terminal. He must have touched the keyboard because the screen had flared to life.

"Looks like the mate bond wasn't the only thing you were researching. Come over here and tell me what all these runes mean." Niall tapped the screen, getting fingerprints on it, but she didn't care.

"They're not runes. They're Zodiac signs." She scrambled upright and joined him. "Did you get us reservations? I wasn't listening."

"Aye, for tonight and the next week. Maybe longer. We'll have to find a place to live, and that might take a wee bit of time." He tapped the screen again. "Interpretation, please."

Her face heated, until she was certain she was bright red. "Um, the base chart is mine. The one overlaying it is yours. I was doing something called synastry, which tells you how well one person will mesh with another."

He wrapped an arm around her waist. "And? What did you discover?"

May as well tell him. No reason to keep it a secret.

"We're about as perfect mates as you could find, although my calculations might be off since your birthday isn't in my computer program, and I had to improvise."

He smiled until his eyes lit with delight. "You could have stopped with perfect mates. No need to add caveats." He turned her until she faced him. "Which did you do first? This or the mate bond dissolution research?"

"Uh, the astrology came first, but I was pissed enough to find out about the other."

"I love your temper—so long as it's not directed my way." He glanced over her shoulder at her office. "I have a suggestion."

"What might that be?" Sarai was fully expecting him to suggest they ditch cleaning in favor of Cora's Inn, something she'd readily agree to since domesticity had never been high on her priority list.

"Let's roll the rug and drag it to the dumpster. Everything else should go fast since you've cleared up most of the splatters."

"I was thinking the same—about the rug."

"See? We are good partners." His kissed her nose and bent to one end of the large rug.

"If you believe in the message embedded in our charts, we kick some serious partner ass."

Niall twisted his head to look at her. "I believe you, darling. Now, give me a hand."

She squatted at the other side of the rug, rolling it toward the door. "You don't really need to help me clean. Once we get the rug out of here."

"How about if I want to?" Warmth crinkled the corners of his eyes. "Maybe I'm collecting chips for when I have a nasty job that would go faster with two of us."

Two of us. She liked the sound of that. Love and heat mingled until she said, "Hurry."

"Aye, darling. Sooner we're done here, the sooner we can get into a shower and scrub ourselves until neither of us stinks of vampire. Once we're clean, we can do...other things."

"Like?" Desire simmered, filling her with a delicious hunger. If she didn't watch it, they'd end up coupling on her floor.

"I'll tell you later."

He hefted his end of the rug, and she got hers. A shot of magic opened her office door and the one leading outside to the trash where they upended the rug into a dumpster.

Sarai hadn't considered the vampire stench problem until he mentioned it. "Geez. I hope they let us into Cora's. I've been inhaling vamp nastiness so long, I've kind of adapted to it." She led the way back to her shop.

"Won't be a problem. I paid for the room and did electronic check-in. We'll teleport into our suite and collect the keys later."

She smiled, pleased he'd planned things out for them.

"What?" He poured a little more bleach into the

bucket, dipped a sponge, and went to work on black blood stains.

"Don't tell anyone, but I could get used to being taken care of." Snapping up the cleaning rag she'd been using, she sluiced it with the bleach solution. "Thanks for not taking me seriously when I told you to get lost."

He turned to look at her. "How could I? We're mates."

"Yes, and I'll come to appreciate what that means as time goes on. Want to know a secret?"

"So long as it comes from your lips, of course."

"There's nothing sexier than a man with a mop or a vacuum or a cleaning rag."

He laughed, rich and low. "I'll keep it in mind, darling."

Her wolf howled; the amulet pulsed, and she got back to work. The sooner they were done, the sooner they could get naked together, and she couldn't wait.

CHAPTER 11

Few Days Later

Niall wrapped a thick, fluffy towel around Sarai, hating to cover her magnificent body but wanting to soak up some of the excess water before they took to the bed. Again.

Cora's Inn was a delightful haven. Furnished with eighteenth century antiques, it was warm and welcoming with dark wood furniture and brocade wall coverings. He'd told Sarai she picked well, but she'd demurred. Said she'd gotten lucky since she'd never seen the inside before.

She dried herself and tossed the towel over a hook. Still naked, she draped the opal amulet around her neck and slipped on the ring and bracelet. The stones blazed bright against her fair skin.

"Does that come-hither look mean it's bedtime?" Her lush mouth spread into an enticing smile.

"It's always bedtime for us. At least until the babies start coming, and then we can paw at each other in a closet or something." His groin tightened with anticipation. He could make love with her nonstop and never tire of her taut breasts, flared hips, and the dark mysteries between her legs.

"I need to get back to work someday. I'll lose all my customers."

"It's nine at night. You can work tomorrow."

Her warm, trilling laugh teased him. He loved to hear her laugh. "Speaking of work," he went on, "I'm transferring to an EMT group in Denver. Lynda gave me a great reference, and I'll be starting soon."

"Thank the goddess." She made cow eyes at him. "At least it will give me time to tend my own business."

"Don't be so certain of that, darling. EMTs work odd hours."

"Eh, so do psychics."

"Well then, it appears another segment of our partnership is destined for success." He made a grab for her, but she evaded him.

Sarai bent to pull the plug on the clawfoot tub. Their suite had both shower and tub, and they'd made good use of both in the few days since they'd settled in.

The globes of her ass parted slightly, giving him a peek at her sex.

Already half hard, his cock shot to full attention, and he surged forward, pinning her against the rim of the tub. He threaded his arms beneath hers and took a breast in each hand, rubbing the already-erect nipples. She made a purring noise deep in her throat and butted her rump against him in obvious invitation.

As he'd suspected, their bodies fit perfectly together for stand-up loving. He transferred a hand between her legs, sliding two fingers inside her. She tightened around him, moaning with delight. Niall bent his head and nipped her shoulder before running his tongue down her spine, slow and lazy.

As she arched into his touch, he let go of the other breast and continued his transit of her silky flesh with his mouth. She tasted of vanilla and honey and musk. The more aroused she got, the more intense her scent and flavor. He'd teased her about being a honeybee in another life, and she'd shrugged and said anything was possible.

He reached the hollow at the base of her spine and sank to his knees behind her, running his tongue down one ass cheek and then the next. He bit and sucked and nipped with her hips rolling from side to side beneath his touch. His cock curved against his belly, achingly hard. The way it was acting, you'd think he hadn't come in weeks instead of just an hour before.

Bending his head to get a better angle, he slid his fingers from her and spread her lips before gliding his tongue into her vault. She reached between her legs and grabbed one of his hands, dragging it forward until his fingers teased her clit.

He knew exactly how she liked to be touched and rubbed her swollen nub with practiced ease in tight little circles. He tongued her as far as he could reach, working her between his hand and his mouth until the hot tide of her climax rained from her. He lapped his reward, waiting until her spasms quieted before drawing her to her feet and turning her to face him.

Her face was splotched with passion. So were her breasts. She closed her mouth over his, teasing his lips with her tongue until he opened to her. He hooked an arm beneath each thigh and lifted her easily so he could slip into her. She wrapped her legs around his waist, never breaking their kiss.

He loved to take her like this, holding her in place with his arms and his cock. She writhed around him, using her legs to lever herself up and down his shaft. He thrust upward, ever willing to help. Her breasts were squashed against his chest, the nipples like hard little agates.

Sex with her was always a wild ride where he

wanted to do everything all at once and had to settle for one thing at time. Right now, he wanted to suckle her breasts and her clit and just look at her, preferably when she had a hand shoved between her legs. She'd been shy about pleasuring herself in front of him, but she'd gotten over it damned fast when he'd stroked himself to a climax in front of her. It made her so hot, she'd stuffed a hand between her legs, frigging herself for all she was worth.

The image heated his blood to molten. He reared back from their kiss, heart thrumming like a tripwire and breath coming in ragged gasps. "I love you, darling."

Her eyes were liquid with lust, her lips soft from their kisses. "Bet you say that to all your wenches."

"Nay. Only you." He lifted her enough to thrust into her. "Ready, darling?"

"More than ready."

She buried her face in his neck and bit hard. The heat of her tantalized him, pushed him so high he was bursting with lust and hunger and a desperate need to care for and protect the woman in his arms. The concentric rhythm of her release drew him along. Semen rushed from him in hot, rough spurts as he clung to her, digging his fingers into her muscled thighs.

They stood like that for long moments, catching

their breath. He nuzzled her neck. "Maybe next time, we'll make it to the bed."

She tilted her head back and grinned. "Why would we want to do that? Put me down."

"Your wish is my command, darling." He lifted her off his erect member and set her on the floor.

She walked to the sink and soaked a washcloth. After drawing it between her legs, she turned and wrapped it around his cock. "Damn. Will it ever be just an ordinary penis again? You know, one that hangs between your legs."

He grabbed the washcloth and chucked it into the sink. "Hush. Don't be wishing such a thing on me." He laced his fingers with hers, and they walked into the bedroom where a king-size bed butted beneath dormer windows.

His phone trilled, and he crossed to the desk to look at the display.

"Don't answer it," Sarai called.

"I have to. It's your uncle." He tapped accept. "Aye? What's going on?"

Stephan's laugh preceded his words. "Very little in my house. I'm sure your life is far more interesting. I called to let you know we're meeting in Golddust tomorrow night—with the mages."

Niall winced. He'd really dropped the ball on that project after he'd told Stephan, Micah, and the other men they'd made a mistake severing ties with their magical cousins.

"Good. I'll be there. What time?"

"Eight."

"Got it. Any more vampire attacks?" Niall almost didn't want to know, but he couldn't hide behind newly mated bliss forever.

"Not here," Stephan spoke slowly, "but there was one in Albuquerque and another in Flagstaff."

Breath whooshed from Niall, and he sank onto a nearby plush chair.

"What is it?" Sarai joined him, sitting in his lap. "Put Uncle on speaker so I can hear."

Niall fiddled with the phone controls.

"Hey, Uncle Stephan," Sarai said.

"Hey yourself. I don't suppose you're ever coming back here, huh?"

"To visit, but Niall and I have been looking for something to rent in town."

"I figured it was something like that," Stephan's voice was gruff. "How about renting from me? It's a big house and mighty lonely without Marie."

Sarai met Niall's gaze, a question in her eyes. He tapped the mute button and asked, "Is that what you want?"

"For now, it would be perfect," she replied. "We

don't exactly have time to house hunt, and Stephan and Marie were very good to me."

Niall unmuted the phone. "Sure and we'd love to take you up on your offer."

"Thank you. Thank you very much. Beyond me being lonely, it's best for shifters to live in groups until we solve the vampire problem."

"Do you think it's solvable?" Sarai asked.

Stephan blew out a noisy breath. "I wish I knew, honey. Depends where their unnatural power is coming from this time."

"Since you brought it up," Niall cut in, "do we have any idea if it's still mage-linked or if the vamps located another patsy?"

"We can float that tomorrow night when we meet with the mages—assuming they're still talking with us."

"It's as good a plan as any. I'm signing off for now," Niall said.

"See you tomorrow," Sarai told her uncle.

"I'll look forward to it, honey."

Niall set the cell phone aside. Worry ate at him. He'd suspected it wouldn't be as easy as killing off a bunch of vampires in Europe to discourage the crew on this side of the Atlantic, but for there to be two more incidents in less than a week was disheartening.

"We'll figure it out." Sarai killed the lights. "Come to bed."

He followed her to the cushy bed a maid had thoughtfully turned down when they'd been out eating dinner. Sarai molded her body to his once they'd laid down, and he cradled her head, stroking her hair.

"I wish we could vanish somewhere, but it's not realistic to shut out the world."

"No," she agreed, "it's not. Shifters need our help."

"I'm selfish enough to want you to be safe."

"What if I feel the same way about you?" she countered. "I fought it, but I love you."

"Och, darling, sure and it's that astrological mumbo-jumbo."

She shook her head where it was cradled in his hands. "My mother used to have a saying."

"What was it?"

"A shifter's mate is in the stars."

He chuckled. "I like it. Was she into psychic pursuits too?"

Sarai tilted her head to look at him in moonlight streaming through their window. "Wait till you meet her. She's a shaman, so I come by my mystical pursuits honestly."

"I thought they lived on the West Coast."

"They do, In Los Angeles, but Stephan told them about our mating—"

"And curiosity took over." Niall finished her

sentence. "When were you going to tell me my new in-laws are on their way?"

"It's not as bad as all that. I only just found out this afternoon—when Mother called to get the details on your astrological chart."

"You could have lied," he said blandly. "Told her I was some sign that never gets along with Cancers."

Sarai shook her head. "Mom is psychic. Remember? You can't pull anything over on her."

"I'll keep it in mind. I suppose they'll be staying with Stephan?"

"Yes, that's the plan."

"We'll wait until they're gone to move in."

She snuggled closer into his embrace. "Smart man. It's one of the reasons I fell for you."

"Oho. You like them smart and handy with a broom, right?"

"You got my number, sweetie. Oh yeah, Mom and Dad should be here day after tomorrow."

Niall thought about the timing. It would be after their powwow with the mages, which was probably good. "How are they traveling?"

"Teleport. How else?"

"Well, they could at least pretend to be human and drive."

Her tone turned serious. "They'll like you. You're a

lot like them in many ways. You probably know my father. He was on that ship with you and Stephan."

"I'll look forward to renewing our acquaintance. Sleep, darling. We haven't been getting very much."

"Only if you rest too."

"I promise."

As her body relaxed against him, he savored the small window of peace they'd carved out for themselves. It wouldn't last. If his jaguar was correct—and the canny bastard was almost never wrong—they'd be in the thick of things again very soon.

Odd the twists and turns life took. He never thought he wanted a mate, but Sarai was the most precious gift in the goddess's world to him. He'd never been one to wish for peace, but he craved it now. His bring-it-on mentality had ceded to staunch protectiveness.

Nothing would harm his mate. Not now. Not ever. He'd do whatever he had to to ensure the vampire-mage coalition went up in smoke. No more long, drawn-out wars. They'd strike hard and fast, killing whoever stood in their way.

The jaguar growled in agreement.

Satisfied he'd done all he could for now, Niall summoned magic and draped a ward around them before he let himself drift into sleep.

You've reached the end of *Gemstone*, kickoff volume for the Wylde Magick series. There's a lot of material to draw from in this world where vampires are on the offensive, draining magic—and blood—where they find it. Look for new Wylde Magick books through the end of 2018 and into 2019.

If you enjoyed this book, you might like my Bitter Harvest series. Full length dystopian urban fantasy featuring shifters and vampires. An excerpt from *Deceived*, first of the Bitter Harvest books, follows.

ABOUT THE AUTHOR

Ann Gimpel is a USA Today bestselling author. A lifelong aficionado of the unusual, she began writing speculative fiction a few years ago. Since then her short fiction has appeared in several webzines and anthologies. Her longer books run the gamut from urban fantasy to paranormal romance. Once upon a time, she nurtured clients. Now she nurtures dark, gritty fantasy stories that push hard against reality. When she's not writing, she's in the backcountry getting down and dirty with her camera. She's published over sixty books to date, with several more planned for 2018 and beyond. A husband, grown children, grandchildren, and wolf hybrids round out her family.

Keep up with her at www.anngimpel.com or http://anngimpel.blogspot.com

If you enjoyed what you read, get in line for special offers and pre-release special reads. Newsletter Signup!

The sea may have been a harsh mistress, but Viktor longs for the challenges of wind and weather, for the sound of waves crashing over his hull. Turned by a Master Vampire, he hates what he's become, but there's no escape. Not from Ushuaia that's turned into a city of bones, or from the Vampire who rules him.

Ketha and eleven other Shifters traveled to Ushuaia to harness the power of an eclipse and were trapped there when the world turned upside down. Ten years later, they're staying one step ahead of Vampires who blame them for the cataclysm.

With her luck running low, Ketha turns her badly depleted magic on the Vampire assigned to lock her away and gets sucked in by her own spell. Maybe magic can't save the world, but love might be able to salvage what's left.

A splintered sign sits under faded wooden archways looking out on Ushuaia Harbor. On the rare clear day, you can still see *El Fin del Mundo*—the end of the world—inscribed on its bleached planks.

The ass end of South America has always been a lonely place, desolate and at the mercy of incessant winds howling through the Tiera del Fuego Mountains. But the sky used to be gray, and the ocean blue. Not anymore. Even the snow isn't white but a murky mixture of puke green and sickly violet. It covers everything year-round since the weather patterns changed too, yielding perpetual winter.

During those early months after the Cataclysm formed an impenetrable blockade around Ushuaia, everyone blamed everybody else. Shifters claimed it was the Vampires' fault. Vamps said Shifters spawned the destruction. Humans caught undercurrents of sketchy magical dealings between Vampires and Shifters, so enchanted trickery may have been the lynchpin that unraveled the world.

After about two years, the blame game played itself out. No one cared anymore, and it didn't up the odds of survival as resources grew scarce.

People—magical and human alike—tried to leave Ushuaia after the Cataclysm. Malevolent tempests—the same ones that turned the sky gray black and the ocean red—attacked everyone who braved the barrier. No one ever returned.

Food and water have become huge problems. Rustic desalination pumps converted salt water until it became too poisonous to consume. Runoff from nearby mountains is suspect, but it's all that's left. Nothing lives in the ocean, and constant storms, coupled with bad water and scarce food, have killed off much of the local animal population.

Locating humans to drain has become close to impossible, so Vampires have grown far less picky, resorting to consuming blood any way they can get it. Soon, not even a rat will be left.

Shifters and humans formed an uneasy alliance in *Ciudad de Huesos*, City of Bones. Neither group trusts the other, but their shared hatred of Vampires has been a potent motivator. Humans barter vegetables for protection and a magical assist from the Shifters so they can keep producing food. Nothing grows without water, though. Sooner rather than later, there will be no more harvests.

City of Bones is an apt name for Ushuaia since its streets are choked with them. Vampires clawed their way to the top of the heap and remained there, their toehold unbreakable. Didn't cost them much. After the Cataclysm, they drained everyone who stood in their way, making new Vamps to swell their ranks and killing those who proved too much trouble. Shifters considered fighting back, but they were too few. As a hedge against unfavorable odds, they concealed themselves with magic and focused their energies on keeping as many humans alive as they could.

"Get out here." Raphael didn't raise his voice. No need. Vampires had exceptional hearing.

Viktor Gaelen hustled into the room where his sire sat at a scarred rolltop desk, checking things off on a list. Fuming at being reduced to little better than a servant, Viktor growled, "What?" Before he got any more words out, a knock boomed from the far end of the suite of rooms.

Viktor sprinted for the door to avoid the temptation to tell Raphael he could find himself another butler. Those conversations never ended well.

Two dark-haired Vampires sauntered inside, their mouths dotted with dried blood. One angled a foot and kicked the door shut. Both stood at attention. Beyond the dried-blood smell, the sour tang of fear oozed from them.

They'd apparently been summoned. No one showed up voluntarily looking as guilty and cowed as this pair.

Viktor nodded their way and headed back toward the bedroom where he'd been calculating one more plan to move himself and a ship he had in dry dock through the barrier holding Ushuaia prisoner. Pages of math equations covered a table where he worked, but he wasn't concerned about Raphael deciphering them. If the old Vampire had gone to school, it was before the birth of modern calculus in the 1600s.

"Where do you think you're going?" Raphael asked in the deadly quiet tone Viktor associated with danger.

"Back there." Viktor jerked his chin at the door leading to the apartment's inner rooms.

"No. You're not."

Viktor didn't reply. Telling his sire to fuck off wasn't on the menu. Those conversations never went well, either.

Raphael stalked to the two Vampires standing near the door, an iron saber trailing from one hand.

Viktor blinked and looked again, wondering if he was hallucinating, but the sword was still there. The blade lived in one of the inner rooms. Raphael must have moved it in anticipation of whatever was about to unfold.

"Where have you two been?" Raphael asked, the

words silky smooth but threaded with the same compulsion Vamps used to lure their victims.

"Here and there," one of the Vampires answered.

"Could you narrow it down?" Raphael took a step nearer his minions.

Viktor balled his hands into fists. He knew what was coming, saw it in the eagerness spilling from his sire. He shouldn't watch, but unless he shut his eyes—a gesture sure to draw Raphael's attention—he didn't have a choice. In addition to being a bloodthirsty pig, Raphael liked an audience.

The other Vampires weren't stupid. In a lightning-fast move, one twisted and made a grab for the doorknob. Before he could turn it, Raphael hefted the blade, swinging it laterally. Its sharp edge cleaved through flesh, bone, and sinew with a sharp cracking sound, and the Vamp's head rolled from his shoulders. Blood sprayed from severed vessels, painting a macabre pattern on the walls and floor.

Viktor breathed shallowly to lessen the stench of blood, shit, and urine, but his stomach still twisted painfully. Bile burned the back of his throat.

The other Vampire fell to his knees, hands clasped in supplication and eyes so wide, white showed all around the irises.

"Where have you been?" Raphael repeated in a bland, conversational tone.

"Feeding from your prisoners. I'm sorry, sire. We were so hungry. It won't happen again. You have my word."

Viktor blanched. Christ. Talk about a capital crime. Why had the Vamps even shown up here? They'd have been better off running for the hills. At least until they hit the barrier.

"Your word isn't worth much." Raphael sounded almost cheerful as he swung the blade a second time.

Viktor stood, rooted in place. Would he be next? Raphael was arbitrary and capricious, and he loved killing.

"Fucking coward. Get moving." Raphael prodded Viktor with the business end of the blade. "Don't let all that blood go to waste. I made them. I can't feed from them, but you can."

Viktor shambled forward, blood hunger doing battle with nausea as he latched onto a geysering carotid. The queasiness would fade. It always did as soon as blood hit his stomach.

"Better." Raphael's voice cut through the haze that settled around Viktor's mind as he fed. "When you're done, clean up the mess." He dropped the sword next to Viktor and returned to his desk as if nothing had happened.

~

Viktor tossed the last bucket of bloody seawater out an open window. He'd had to hustle water up from the bay, two buckets at a time, cursing Raphael with every single step. Other Vamps had shown up and claimed the corpses, hauling them off to finish draining them elsewhere. Viktor had struck a deal with them. Blood in exchange for transport. It simplified his cleaning chores.

Raphael hadn't moved from his desk. He dipped an old-fashioned quill pen into an inkwell filled with something murky and continued with whatever he was writing.

Viktor glanced at the ornate iron sword he'd balanced against one wall after cleaning blood off its blade. He wanted nothing more than to snatch it up and behead his sire. Wanting and doing were two different things, though. According to Vampire lore, hideous consequences would ensue if he had the balls to raise so much as his little finger against the one who'd made him.

Raphael set the pen down and stood. He paced from one side of the lavishly decorated room to the other, his silence more menacing than idle conversation would have been. In the years since Viktor had become Raphael's minion, he'd observed three basic modes: patronizing lectures, blood frenzy, and silence. The latter was the worst because it was hard to gauge what lay behind it.

Or what would come next.

Lightning blitzed across the corner of his vision, splitting a sky that had shaded to dark gray. Muted booms rocked the building. Was today when it would finally crumble, joining several of Ushuaia's other multistory structures in rubble choking the streets? He lived in this building, but in an ancient sub-basement that backed onto an equally ancient tunnel system. The main reason he'd chosen his damp, subterranean abode, putting up with a windowless room that was never truly warm, was because the intricate warren of passageways offered an escape route. At least he wouldn't wake some evening trapped beneath tons of concrete and twisted rebar.

His sire was in a foul mood, particularly considering his two kills, but the silent standoff was getting to Viktor. He took a chance and cleared his throat.

"What?" The other Vampire stood and spun to face his spawn.

It was easy to see where he'd gotten his name. Beautiful as any angel, Raphael's hair swirled around him to waist level in a silky, dark cloud. A high forehead and square jaw framed fangs that were extended, probably because he was hungry. Like everyone else in *Ciudad de Huesos*, Raphael sported a collection of skins and rags hanging off his lean frame. Vampires—at least the original variety like Raphael— didn't notice the cold as much as other races, but the ever-present chill sank into everyone's bones after a while.

His blue-gray eyes shot darts at Viktor. "What?" he repeated.

"How'd you find out about the two poachers? Did someone rat on them?"

Raphael snorted laughter. "I don't require informants. I know everything about each of my minions."

"Of course, Sire. Didn't mean to suggest otherwise." Viktor regarded his sire with as direct a gaze as he could muster. He'd gotten away with a whole lot, which meant Raphael was lying about knowing everything. He didn't. Not by a long shot. Not that Viktor had done anything quite as egregious as drinking from Raphael's private stock, but almost.

"You missed a spot." Raphael pointed at a spray of crimson decorating one wall near the floor.

Viktor shrugged. "You need a maid. I'll get it later. You called the Tribunal into session. They'll be waiting for you."

Raphael spat saliva mixed with blood onto the cold hearth. "Let the bastards wait. I'm Nosferatu."

Viktor clung to his neutral expression. He hadn't even known Vampires existed before Raphael captured him, and he'd turned a deaf ear to his sire's constant nattering about Nosferatu this and Nosferatu that. When he'd dug into Raphael's neglected but considerable library, he'd discovered Vampires actually emerged from an alliance between the devil and Sekhmet, Egyptian goddess of death and slaughter. He'd never bothered to mention that to Raphael. No reason to dispute the old fucker's delusions about his origins.

Viktor stood straighter. "There's the matter of the Shifter we captured—"

Raphael made a chopping motion. "Enough. I don't require reminding. All the Shifters have been a thorn in our sides for a long time. We have to kill them. If we'd done that before the Cataclysm, we wouldn't be in this unspeakable mess."

"But there weren't any Shifters here before the Cataclysm—" Viktor held up a hand. "Sorry. Didn't mean to contradict you."

Raphael stalked closer, dripping arrogance. "Of course, there were. You wouldn't have known about them—or us."

"True enough," Viktor muttered.

Raphael's nostrils flared, and he added, "We have to locate them. No more excuses. They'll make a substantial addition to our food stocks, and I tire of sustaining myself on animal blood."

Viktor opened his mouth to point out they'd been searching for the Shifters for years without so much as a clue, but Raphael knew that. Vampires might have supernatural strength and speed, but Shifters commanded a far greater array of magical ability.

"What are you thinking?" Raphael narrowed his eyes.

"Nothing. You were saying?"

Raphael snapped his fingers, clearly struck by a revelation.

Viktor waited to see what atrocity his sire was cooking up now. To mask his aversion to Raphael's ideas—not a minion-like reaction at all—he glanced around the room. Carved wainscoting circled the walls, and high cove ceilings held delicate paintings left from an earlier era, before the world shifted on its axis, trapping them in the few square miles around what had once been the southernmost seaport in the world.

"It would be perfect," his sire went on, oblivious to Viktor's inner conflict. "Definitely a win-win solution. With Shifters out of the way, their magic will fade. Absent their protective spells, we'd be able to locate the humans." He swiped his palms together. "Problem solved. Between humans and Shifters, they'll feed us for a long time—provided we're careful and don't drain them to the point of death."

Viktor muttered something noncommittal.

"Don't you see?" Raphael swung to face him. "We'd develop a system so some would always be ready. Once they were up to snuff, we'd feed from them again. We did something similar back in the Middle Ages when life was cheap, and no one ever complained about a missing relative or two."

"What do you plan to feed them, Sire? So they don't die." Viktor should have kept his mouth shut, but it was an important question.

"They'll eat whatever's keeping them alive now," Raphael sputtered. "It's a perfect plan that will provide a perpetual food source for us." He narrowed his eyes to slits. "Whose side are you on?"

"Ours, Sire. Who else's?" Viktor ginned up an earnest expression and hoped Raph didn't question him further. Vampires were decent at sniffing out lies.

Sidestepping the specter of genocide for Shifters and humans, mostly because he figured they'd all be dead—Shifters, Vamps, humans, and anyone who'd remained in the shadows—before too many more months passed, Viktor said, "Perhaps we'd be better served harnessing Shifter power to address the poisoned water. They must be doing something, or the humans wouldn't still be growing crops to sustain themselves."

Raphael rounded on him, the noxious, rotten-egg stench of hungry Vampire thickening by the moment. "Intriguing idea about detoxifying the water. Those crops will keep the humans alive, so they'll last longer for us to feed on."

Viktor didn't bother pointing out that securing the Shifters' cooperation for anything was unlikely. He switched topics to move Raphael away from killing and death, his two favorite themes. "Do you suppose there's any life left beyond the storms that hold us captive here? I used to tap into radio broadcasts until electricity dwindled to almost nothing. The last few times I tried, though, I couldn't find any left on the air."

Raphael's eyes sharpened with sudden cunning, a harsh reminder how ancient and powerful he was. "Why would you ask about life beyond Ushuaia? Does it have something to do with that indecipherable chicken scratch back at your worktable?"

"Same reason you highlighted with your plans for the Shifters and humans. We're running out of food. That's what my calculations are about. Resource allocation." Viktor hoped to hell Raphael couldn't read his mind. He'd been fishing for information to see how viable his plan to breach the barrier with his ship would be.

Raphael didn't know about *Arkady*, and Viktor aimed to keep it that way.

Vampires weren't particularly blessed with magic. Not that they couldn't intuit the odd thought and light fires and do other sleight of hand parlor tricks, but magic had a price. Most Vamps were too depleted from not having fed properly for years to squander any energy on superfluous activities.

His sire resumed pacing, tension evident in his straight back and precise stride. "Yes, there's life outside Ushuaia. Of course, there is. There has to be."

Viktor held a neutral expression. Raphael had no idea. His answer was sheer bluff, or he'd have tossed out facts to back up his statements. Maybe it would be easier to rid himself of Raphael than he'd thought.

Who am I kidding? He may not know shit about what's beyond the barrier, but he knows a whole lot more about being a Vampire than I ever will. I'd do well not to underestimate that part.

Raphael altered his back-and-forth path and walked close enough to thump Viktor's chest with an extended index finger. "It's the Shifters' fault. All of this. They hold magic to see beyond the barrier."

"If that's accurate, maybe it's not in our best interest to kill them," Viktor ventured. If Shifters truly held information that could help them or the ability to make their water resources last longer, it was worth challenging Raphael.

A long, sibilant sound slithered from between Raphael's perfectly formed lips. "What good is knowledge if we can't breach the barrier? Look at that." He trotted to a grimy window and pointed outside at lightning flares striking the red-tinged ocean. Every place they hit, the ocean bubbled around them, as if it were claiming the energy, absorbing it to make certain its waters turned even more lethal. "I've been alive for a long time, and I've never seen its like, nor anything remotely close."

Viktor shrugged. There had to be a way to get around the barrier. Some complex escape hatch no one had discovered yet, but he kept his mouth shut. Raphael didn't appreciate vague concepts without facts to back them up. It was how Viktor had known his assertion about life outside Ushuaia was speculation.

"The Tribunal?" Viktor gestured toward the door.

"You're worse than a social secretary," Raphael grumbled and walked briskly out of the room.

Viktor snatched up a ratty jacket woven from llama skins and slid into it before following his sire. He had warm clothing aboard his ship, but explaining where it came from would be a problem. Every shop in Ushuaia had been looted years ago. Raphael would notice any deviation from "normal," and he'd ask questions until

Viktor came up with a satisfactory answer. Better to dress in rags like everybody else.

Raphael had turned him a few months after the Cataclysm converted Ushuaia into a prison. He hadn't particularly wanted to be a Vampire. Raphael had forced his will onto him, much as he'd muscled his way through five hundred years of feeding and swelling the ranks of his Vampire tribe.

Back then—pre-Cataclysm—there'd been a whole lot more humans. Viktor had been a cruise ship captain on his way to the Falkland Islands when a tsunami drove his boat into the South American coast, fetching it up on deadly rocks. He'd done his best to save his passengers and crew. In the end, he'd herded the fifty who were left out of nearly a hundred across brutal coastal mountains and into Ushuaia. Only to find it taken over by Vampires.

Vampires.

Who would've thought something like that was even real?

Worse, Vamps captured them immediately and transported them to a mountain cave system with primitive cells, probably built by some iteration of indigenous hunter-gatherers. Viktor had spent months there, long enough to curse his stupidity waltzing into Ushuaia unprotected. Long enough to discover Shifters also existed, and that Vamps hated them. Long enough to hear about the Cataclysm that shattered the world.

Long enough to stop caring what happened.

And more than long enough to be disappointed when another morning dawned and he wasn't dead yet. Turning into a Vampire hadn't changed a damned thing on that front. But it did make it much harder for him to die.

Viktor pelted down stairs falling into disrepair. Raphael was a long way ahead of him, and he didn't particularly want to attract his sire's attention.

Master Vampires were old and strong. According to Raphael, his particular type of Vampire stood at the top of the heap. Princes or kings or something. They took what they wanted and created a legion of Vampires to stand by their sides. Something about the draining and resurrection created loyalty to one's sire. It was supposed to, anyway.

Viktor swallowed back a bitter taste. He could feel the bond to Raphael like a tightly coiled spring deep in his belly, and he resented the hell out of it. Over the nine plus years since his making, he'd experimented with ways to break away from Raphael, but nothing ever worked.

It was why he cast longing glances at the iron saber. Maybe if he were quick enough, he could circumvent the bond.

He'd have to be goddamned fast, though. And successful. Punishment would be swift and certain if Raphael suspected his devotion wasn't absolute. He'd considered talking with some of Raphael's other minions to sow the seeds of a rebellion, but fear always stayed his tongue, and he hated himself for his cowardice.

Cold hit him like a wall as he left the building where they lived and hustled across a debris-choked walkway to their council chambers. Abandoned cars littered the streets. Ushuaia had no fossil fuels or refineries. All the gasoline had been trucked in. Once it ran out, cars became useless. Because he wasn't paying attention, he tripped over a pile of bones, the remains of some unlucky humans who hadn't survived either the Cataclysm or a Vamp feeding frenzy. Bones lay everywhere, bleached by incessant storms and stripped by animal predators desperate for a meal.

Dead people.

Dead cars.

Death extended on all sides of him. He shouldn't give a shit. Vampires didn't feel pain or sorrow or loss, but he still did. Setting his jaw in a hard, tight line, Viktor buried emotions that ran far too close to the surface.

Even though he didn't inhale deeply, the frigid air still bit deep, smelling a shred more poisonous than it had the day before. He stole a glance at the sky. Sunlight eroded Vampire abilities, but it wasn't a problem here. Though he was certain the sun still sat in judgment over the planet, its presence over Ushuaia was rare.

"You were the one in a hurry," Raphael scoffed from the shadows of carved double doors.

"So I was. Sorry." Viktor joined his sire, grateful when the doors clanked shut behind them, sealing out some of the cold.

Raphael sent a penetrating look his way before starting the trek to the tenth floor. Electricity was in short supply. What little they had came from wind farms, hastily expanded during the early years after the Cataclysm. Humans had overseen their growth and run them, but they'd abandoned the farms once they became a prime target for Vampire abductions. Without ongoing attention, the wind farms were falling to ruin like everything else. When juice flowed, Viktor used his tiny allocation to heat his quarters. Sometimes he envied the older, colder-blooded Vamps. They didn't require warmth in quite the same way he did.

More to divert his attention from the endless, winding stairs than anything else, he asked, "Any idea why you—" He stumbled over his words, and tried again. "Why I feel the cold more intensely than you?"

It was an inane question, but Viktor was curious what his sire would say.

Raphael twisted his classic features into a sneer. "It's the Shifters' fault. Everything is. They perverted our power and used it to augment their own. Beyond that, you're not a pure blood straight from the old country."

"Does that mean if you'd found me before I left Germany and turned me there—?"

"Enough. Do not question me."

Viktor dropped behind his sire to avoid any possibility of eye contact. He'd eat his socks if Raphael knew any more about Vampires than he did. Probably a whole lot less, given his discovery about the unholy alliance between the devil and Sekhmet creating Vamps in the first place. All that Nosferatu crap was a smoke and mirrors act. Plus, there was no fucking way Shifters could have had shit to do with new Vamps being more susceptible to cold. Those changes had to be a corollary of the Cataclysm and its perversion of the energies that used to keep the world in balance.

One more flight and they'd be there. Viktor wasn't winded. Vamps were strong, but he needed to do more. Short rations and little exercise made him slower than he should've been.

Raphael trotted down a long, dark hallway, with Viktor at his heels and pushed into the space they used for the Tribunal. Ten Vamps shot to their feet, waiting for Raphael to stride to the front of the room. Once upon a time, this particular oval-shaped chamber had been a chapel on the top floor of a hospital. It still held a simple elegance with painted sconces and wooden benches arranged around a central nave. A bronze Christ figure hung from the far wall, his sightless eyes gazing disapprovingly on what had become of a once-sacred place.

Viktor quashed a temptation to genuflect before the icon and faded to one side, standing next to Juan Torres, the closest thing he had to a friend within Vampire ranks. They'd worked on the same ship before the Cataclysm. Even though they didn't spend much together, it was more because Vampires weren't into *social* than any other reason.

The coppery stench of blood rose from where Raphael bent over a large, squirming rat one of his minions had thoughtfully provided. Viktor's mouth flooded with saliva, and he swallowed fast before it dripped down his chin.

The rat squealed, vocalizing horror as life drained from its gray, furry body. Viktor gave himself a sharp mental slap. For some reason, the transition from human to monster hadn't been as effective in him because he still thought in human terms. Concepts like manners and compassion and sensitivity weren't anywhere in the Vampire lexicon.

Juan elbowed him surreptitiously and shot a pained glance his way. Before Viktor could mine for details, the chapel door slapped against its stops. Two more Vamps dragged an unconscious woman into the room. Iron manacles bound her wrists and ankles, so she had to be the Shifter they'd captured.

Viktor had never laid eyes on her before, and he fought to hide his reaction to her beauty. Long dark hair shot with red and gold dragged on the floor. Her eyes were closed, but sculpted cheekbones dusted with freckles showcased full, red lips. Tall and broad-shouldered, she moaned incoherently as the Vamps manhandled her to where Raphael stood.

Rat still in one hand, Raphael eyed the Shifter. Blood dripped down his chin and onto the floor. Not only was Raphael eating in front of them, he was squandering some of his meal. Viktor fought an inane desire to race to those fallen, crimson blobs and lick them up. Never mind he'd just fed.

Damn it!

He had to get a better grip on his emotions. Vamps, the ones where the turning worked, anyway, didn't experience much beyond hunger, desire, and anger. They'd moved past fear and caring and the rest of it. So what if Raphael was an insensitive boor? Vamps didn't view the world through that lens.

"Drop her there," Raphael ordered.

His voice broke into Viktor's churning thoughts.

The Shifter's body made a *splatting* sound when her two escorts did as ordered before withdrawing to where the other Vamps spread throughout the chapel. Viktor's nostrils twitched at an unusual scent. It took a moment to understand he was smelling the Shifter's blood. It reminded him of wildflowers and the stunted Antarctic beech trees that used to grow in the *Tiera del Fuego*. The scent drew him, soothed him, made him feel whole again, not splintered into a no-man's land where he no longer knew himself. Not exactly Vamp, but not human, either.

He clasped his hands behind his back, squeezing hard to avoid the temptation to kneel next to her and cradle her head in his arms, smoothing stray strands of bright hair away from her grime-streaked face. Most of all, he wanted to get her away from Raphael before the Master Vampire decided to try to turn her. If that didn't work, she'd end up a meal—or many meals, depending how long they could keep her alive.

The thought disgusted him. She was perfect. One of nature's creations. The magic seeping from her—despite her iron manacles—wrapped her in an iridescent shroud that felt pure, decent. He hadn't had much congress with Shifters, but none he'd run across felt anything like the woman sprawled on the floor. Granted, he'd only seen them from a distance, but still...

He clamped his hands together harder before one of his Vampire kin noticed the unrest that had to be streaming from him. To be on the safe side, he shuttered his thoughts, burying them deep.

Raphael nudged the woman with one booted foot. As decrepit as the rest of his clothing, his boots weren't much more than strips of dried-out leather secured by duct tape. The Shifter moaned, and Raphael hauled off and kicked her.

Viktor clamped his jaws together so hard he feared his teeth would crack. If he'd had any inkling the Shifter would kindle something inside him, an awareness he'd been certain died along with his humanity, he'd never have—

Never would have, what? His mental voice inquired caustically.

For some unexplained reason, he was one of Raphael's favorites, and the Master Vamp rarely went anywhere without Viktor by his side. Leaving was out of the question. He had to wait this out. Soon enough, he could retire to his grotto beneath the building across the street. Maybe fortune would smile on him, and it would collapse, trapping Raphael in rubble that might take years to dig out of.

Fat chance. That fucker is strong as sin—

A low groan drew Viktor's attention back to the Shifter. She'd rolled to a sitting position, and her eyes were open. A fine, clear golden color, they formed slits as she stared defiantly at Raphael.

"You've captured me, Vampire," she sneered, displaying very white, very even teeth. "Now what? Do I get to be everyone's dinner?" She swung her head from side to side, encompassing the room full of Vamps. "At least remove my shackles. If I'm going to die, I'd rather face you as a wolf."

Thick black robes, sashed in brilliant red, clung to her slender frame, but the fabric was whole, not patched. Could Shifters leverage magic to repair simple things like that? Viktor wished he knew. His only information about other magical beings came from hearsay and rumors—and Raphael's library. A long-standing Vampire rule, though, was no interaction with Shifters under any circumstances.

No one had ever explained why, and he'd never cared enough to ask.

Until now.

He inhaled sharply, and then did it again. Maybe filling his lungs would spur his turbulent thoughts into something beyond chasing their own tails. Would

Raphael follow through on his threat to kill the Shifter and the rest of her kind? Or would he glom onto Viktor's idea about using their magic to counteract the increasingly bad water?

"My name is Ketha." She flowed to her feet in a single, graceful motion and folded her arms beneath the swell of her breasts. "Rat got your tongue?" She jerked her chin at the dead rat still clutched in Raphael's hand and skinned her lips back from her teeth.

Before Raphael could answer, she went on. "If you're going to kill me, get on with it, but know this—" Her voice took on a mesmerizing quality, and magic rose in waves around her, turning the air shimmery with color. "You will never escape Ushuaia without us."

Raphael faced off against her. "What makes you think we want to escape, Shifter?"

Ketha shrugged, favoring the Vampire with the full force of her golden gaze. "You like it here? Soon there won't be anything left to eat or drink, and then all of us will die. Even Vampires. But if you're good with that"—another eloquent shrug—"I suppose there's nothing to talk about. Go on." She made shooing motions with one long-fingered hand. "Get on with it. I'm prepared to die. We don't have too many more months here at the ass end of the world before none of us will be left. Take a chance, Vampire. Face me as a wolf."

Viktor knew his sire well and recognized barely suppressed rage in the set of his shoulders and the cold, dead aspect to his expression.

"I'll pass. I suppose you have the answer to all our problems." Raphael quirked a well-formed dark brow.

A small, secretive smile played about Ketha's mouth. "Even if I did, I'd never tell you. Funny thing about being captured. It quiets the tongue."

"Show some respect. No one addresses me like that."

"It appears I just did." Ketha tossed her shoulders back, bringing her to a height with the Vampire, and a snarl rose from her throat. "You need us. Unfortunately, we need you as well, but what I had in mind was equal partners at a conference table, not being knocked over the head and dragged here."

A vein throbbed in Raphael's temple. Small cracking sounds rose from the rat as he crushed it in one hand, splattering blood and entrails across the white marble floor.

"Viktor." Raphael wasn't looking his way, but the summons was clear.

"Sire?" Viktor's gut twisted with apprehension. What would come next? Would he be assigned some grisly assassination? Worse, would he be ordered to feed from the creature staring down the room with her unnerving gaze?

If that happened, and he ended up guzzling her blood, he'd never be able to live with himself. It had been hard enough feeding on what was left after other Vamps had drained humans. Whoever he'd once been would be irretrievably lost if Raphael forced him to kill the Shifter or drink her blood.

What the fuck is wrong with me? Not a Vamp. Not human. Not anything at all but trapped in a place I once considered home—when I wasn't at sea.

"Get up here!" Raphael thundered.

Viktor trotted smartly to his side.

Whatever this was, he wanted it over with. Then he'd take the iron blade and do what he should've done long ago. Damn the consequences. His life wasn't worth shit. Why prolong it? And maybe, just maybe, he'd manage to do away with Raphael. At least then he could live out however many months he had left free from his sire's oppressive yoke.

Raphael drew a set of old-fashioned handcuffs from one of his many pockets. Moving faster than a human eye could follow, the Vamp snapped cuffs on Ketha right behind the wrist manacles. "Take her to the caves," he said and all but pushed her into Viktor's arms.

Viktor latched a hand firmly around Ketha's elbow.

Her intoxicating scent filled his nose, but he ignored it. "What then?" he asked Raphael.

His sire sent an incredulous look his way. "Lock her up and return. I'll decide her fate once she's told us what she knows about escaping Ushuaia."

"I already explained how that would happen." Ketha's tone was pointed. "At a conference table as an equal. So long as you hold me captive, my wolf and I will die before we help you do anything."

Raphael slanted his gaze her way. "It appears we're at a stalemate. Perhaps some cell time will alter your perspective."

"Don't count on it."

Relief weakened Viktor's knees, but he did his damnedest to hide the excitement sluicing through him. He didn't have to kill Ketha. Didn't have to do a thing beyond delivering her to the prison caves. He'd leave her in the cell he'd occupied because it was farthest from the ravages of the poisoned ocean and more comfortable than the others.

An insidious thought intruded. Before he could stop himself, a treasonous path stretched dead ahead. He'd know where she was, which meant he could free her. In truth, he never had to lock her up at all. Too late, he felt the subtle edges of her magic probe his mind. He engaged wards, but a smile turned her face into something profanely beautiful.

"Lead out." She hip-butted him. "This room stinks of Vampires, and it's giving me a headache."

Raphael snarled and lunged for her. He grabbed her shoulders and shook her until her teeth rattled against each other. "Keep a civil tongue in your head, or I'll rethink my generosity. Never forget who runs things in Ushuaia. This is blood's dominion. *My* dominion."

Ketha stood her ground. "Funny, but I thought I and my Shifters were in charge. Besides, if you were going to kill me, I'd already be dead."

Viktor tamped down growing admiration for the woman. As soon as Raphael let go, he hustled her out of the room.

"Remain quiet." He kept his tone stern and herded her toward the stairwell. "Vampires have excellent hearing."